SECRETS

MOUNTAIN

Another You Say Which Way Adventure
by:

BLAIR POLLY & DM POTTER

ISBN-13:978-1519181671
ISBN-10:1519181671

How This Book Works

- This story depends on YOU.

- YOU say which way the story goes.

- What will YOU do?

At the end of each chapter, you get to make a decision. Turn to the page that matches your choice. **P62** means turn to page 62.

There are many paths to try. You can read them all over time. Right now, it's time to start the story. Good luck.

Oh … and watch out for morph rats!

SECRETS OF GLASS MOUNTAIN

In the beginning.

With the screech of diamonds on smooth black rock, a troop of Highland Sliders comes skidding to a stop ten yards from you and your schoolmates.

"That's what I want to do when I graduate," says Dagma. "Being a Highland Slider looks like so much fun."

Another classmate shakes his head. "Yeah, but my cousin went mining and struck it rich on his first trip out. Now he owns two hydro farms and his family live in luxury."

You look around the small settlement where you grew up. It's a beautiful place, high on the Black Slopes of Petron. Far below, past the sharp ridges and towering pinnacles, the multicolored fields of the Lowlands stretch off into the distance. At the horizon, a pink moon sits above a shimmering turquoise sea.

But the beauty isn't enough to keep you here. You could never be a farmer or a merchant. You've always dreamed of travel and adventure.

Maybe mining is the right thing to do. You imagine heading off into the wild interior looking for diamonds and the many secrets these glass mountains contain. Imagine striking it rich!

Or do you become a slider like so many others from your family? What would happen to your home without the protection of the Highland Sliders? How would people move around the dangerous slopes from settlement to settlement without their expert guidance? And who would stop the Lowlanders from invading?

Your part in this story is about to begin. You will leave school at the end of the week and it's time for you to choose your future.

It is time to make your first decision. Do you:

Start cadet training to become a slider? **P3**

Or

Go to mining school so you can go prospecting? **P75**

You have decided to start cadet training to become a slider.

"Eyes front, cadets!" the uniformed officer yells. "If you are going to become sliders you'd better listen like your life depends on it, because believe me, it does." The officer stamps a heavy boot for effect and scans your group "You've all made it through basic training, now it's time to see if you have what it takes to become true Highland sliders."

You knew this part of cadet training was going to be tough, but this officer looks like he eats black glass for breakfast. His dome shaped skull is covered in scars and half his right ear is missing.

You squirm on the hard stone bench and give the girl next to you a weak smile. The room is full of young cadets and like you, they all look a little scared.

Your stomach feels like it is full of moon moths. You cross your fingers and hope you won't let your family down.

"Right, you lot, I want to see you all at the top of the training slope in ten minutes. Anyone who's not there when the bell goes may as well slide right over and enroll in mining school. Now let's go cadets, move it!"

You stand up and quick march out of the room with the others. You've seen the training area from below with its shadowed gullies, crevasses, and sharp ridges, but you are about to look down upon its glistening black slopes for the first time.

4

You are third to arrive. You check the strap leading from your tow clamp to the belt of your harness and make sure everything is connected properly. As you line up for the tow, more moths have come to join their friends fluttering in your belly.

You point your front foot forward, and engage the metal rod that locks your boots together to form a stable platform for you to slide on. Then you bend your knees in readiness for a high-speed, uphill ride.

The towpath looks slightly damp and you know the black rock will be slipperier than the smoothest ice. The towline whirls around a big, motorized wheel downhill from where you are standing before it extends up the mountainside and disappears into a purple fog. You know there is another wheel at the top that takes the cable and sends it back down the hill again, but you won't be able to see that one until you've gained some altitude.

After flipping your tow clamp over the rapidly moving cable you gradually squeeze its handles together and slowly increase the pressure. Before you know it you are accelerating. The cable hums and vibrates as it drags you uphill. Wind whistles across your visor and around your helmet. You taste the dampness of the mist.

The two cadets on the towline ahead of you stand with knees slightly bent, their front feet pointed forward, their back feet angled slightly to one side. Lock-rods hold their boots just the right distance apart for maximum control. But despite months of training on the simulator, their knees still wobble a little.

You are a little unsteady on your feet too, but you figure this is caused as much by nervous anticipation as anything. When you relax a little, you find you do better. Fighting the tow just makes your leg muscles ache. You remember what the instructors have said about letting the cable do the work. You lean back into your harness and let it take your weight. As you do, you feel your legs relax.

You feel every bump and irregularity through the soles of your boots as you slide along, allowing you to make subtle corrections of balance. You must keep alert to remain upright.

The fog thins as you gain altitude. The top wheel comes into view and you know that in the next twenty seconds or so you will have to disengage your tow clamp and slide off the path onto the staging area. A clean dismount is all a matter of timing.

There are instructors at the top of the hill ready to grade your efforts. You disengage your tow clamp, hook it over a loop on your utility belt and spread your arms slightly to stay balanced.

You shoot off the tow a bit hot, but adjust your speed by lifting the toe of your leading foot a little, dragging the spike fitted to your heel into the rocky slope. A high-pitched squeal fills the air as the diamond digs into the surface and slows you down.

When you come to a stop, you release your back foot, kick the lock-rod back into the sole of your boot and stand to attention.

"Well done, cadet," an instructor says. "You've been listening to the lectures I see."

"Thank you sir," you say, snapping off a quick salute.

With a screech, the next cadet slides in and stands beside you. Others cadets arrive at the staging area every ten seconds or so until there are three rows of ten cadets standing shoulder to shoulder.

The cadet next to you is a tall boy with clear blue eyes. "Ready for the slide of your life?" he says with confidence.

You nod to the boy. "I think so. Bit late now if I'm not."

You are as ready as you will ever be. After all, you have been training for this day for the last year with classes during the day and practice on the simulator every night. You've had guide stick training, terrain training, balance training, combat training. You've studied geometry, navigation and communications. Now it's time to put everything into practice and have your first run under real conditions.

"Right cadets, it is time to show us what you're made of," the training officer says. He takes a step forward and points to the scars on his head. "I got these on my first run when I missed a turn and ended up crashing into the lip of an overhanging ridge. If you think my head looks bad, you should have seen the helmet I was wearing. I suggest you concentrate so you don't make a similar mistake." The officer looks along the line. "First one to the bottom will be promoted to troop leader. Are you ready?"

"Yes sir!" the cadets yell in unison.

"Right, line up and get ready to slide."

Shuffling forward, you stand near the edge, ready to leap off the narrow shelf onto the much steeper slope below. You look left, then right.

You've gotten to know the strengths and weaknesses of each cadet over the months of basic training. Your strongest competition is a stocky girl named Dagma from a neighboring community. Dagma doesn't like to finish second.

Gagnon, a tall boy with short spiky hair and pale green eyes nods in your direction. "Good luck," he says.

"Luck's got nothing to do with it." Dagma snarls. "Sliding is about skill. If you're going to rely on luck you should take up mining."

You look at Gagnon, and roll your eyes. Dagma can be such a grunter at times.

"Lock boots!" the instructor orders.

You release the lock-bar from the sole of your left boot and attach it to a fitting near the instep of your right. You hear a satisfying click as it snaps into place. You now have a rigid platform to slide on.

The instructor hands each of you a guide stick. "These are worth more than you are, so don't lose them."

The guide stick is almost as tall as you are. Its shaft is made from a flexible and incredibly strong wood obtained by trading crystals with the border tribes. Mounted on one end of the shaft is a sturdy blue-diamond hook. On the stick's opposite end is a thick pad of tyranium needle crystals.

The ultra-fine tyranium crystals create friction when dragged on the ground. This friction is used to control a slider's direction and speed when moving down the slope.

You rest the pad end on the ground and immediately feel how the crystals grip the glossy black surface. It's no wonder they are only fractionally less prized than blue diamonds. Without them it would be virtually impossible to travel, harvest eggs from the red-beaked pango colonies, drill mines and reservoirs, or build sleeping and hydro growing pods.

The instructor stands tall and barks out orders. "Are you ready cadets?"

You lower your visor and work your front foot as close to the edge as possible. Gripping the guide stick tightly in both hands, you rest it on the ground behind you. Now, the slightest push will send you plunging down the hill. The other cadets crowd together, bumping shoulders, hoping to achieve the most favorable slide path down the centre of the course.

You look down the run. There are gullies and ridges, knobs and small pillars. Some parts are near vertical, others flatten out only to drop steeply again when you least expect it.

The most popular line runs down the side of a steep ridge and then sweeps into a broad valley on the right hand side of the course. At the bottom of the valley it angles back towards the centre, cuts below two small pinnacles and then straightens towards the finish line. All the cadets have studied the course map and know the relative advantages and dangers of the various ways down.

The instructor raises his arm. "On my mark! Ready to drop in five, four, three, two, one…" His arm falls. "Slide!"

With a firm push you are over the edge and sliding. You squat low to create less wind resistance and tap the needle end of your stick to make subtle course corrections.

Dagma's strong push has her leading the pack, sliding smoothly to your right. The other cadets are sticking to her tail, trying to gain advantage by using her bulk as a wind shield.

Gagnon is near the front as well, sliding effortlessly, but unless Dagma makes a mistake it will be hard to pass her. It looks as though the other cadets have chosen to take the conventional and less risky route down the mountain.

You've seen the times posted on the classroom wall and know the winner of this race for the last three years has taken this route. But you also know that crowded slopes are dangerous. Each year at least one cadet has been badly injured after being bumped off course.

During your study of the map, you've seen an untried route that runs between the two small pinnacles in the centre of the main face. It's risky, but if you can turn sharply enough, you just might be able to enter the narrow chute at a point above the two small pillars, and take a straighter, faster line to the finish.

However, if you misjudge your timing, and miss the turn into the top of the chute, you could end up in a gulley of dangerous ripples. If that happens and you lose your footing, these ripples will slice you to ribbons.

You are sliding fast. If you are going to try to make the turn you will have to do it now. You've practiced this move plenty of times on the simulator, but in real life conditions, nothing is guaranteed. You look right, then left. It's now or never.

It is time to make a quick decision. Hurry! Do you:

Go for it and try to turn into the chute, despite the danger? **P11**

Or

Follow Dagma and the others and try to win the race using the normal route? **P15**

You have decided to go for the chute despite the danger.

Making sharp turns on a slope of black glass isn't easy. Luckily you've had plenty of practice on the simulator.

You stand up tall and spread your arms. Special pockets of fabric, where your arms meet your torso, catch the wind and slow you down a little. Then you swivel your hips and drop your diamond hook. A three-second drag slows you down even more. Once you've lost enough momentum, you flip your guide stick around and repeatedly stab the ground with the needle crystal end. Each time the crystals hit the surface, you move a little to your left.

Looking ahead, you try to spot the entrance of the narrow chute leading down between the two pinnacles. On the shiny black surface it's difficult to see the contours. It should be coming up about…

You spot it, but you're too far left! More jabs of your stick move you back to the right. As you stare ahead, sweat drips down your forehead into your visor. You are on the correct line now. You crouch to regain speed. Your arms and guide stick are tucked tight to your body.

Flying over the lip at the top of the chute the ground falls away and you lose contact with the slope. As you drop into the steeply angled half-pipe, you rise slightly from your crouch and hold the guide stick out in front of you, using it to help keep your balance. If you are going to win the race, you must stay on your feet.

When your boots touch the ground you drop into a tuck and streamline your body. Momentum takes you up one side of the half-pipe and then gravity brings you back to the bottom.

You are really moving now, going faster than you've ever experienced on the simulator. Wow, what a feeling! You look down the slope. It's a straight run to the bottom.

Moments later, you flash across the finish line and drop your hook. But are you the first to arrive?

"What are you smiling about cadet?" the instructor at the bottom of the course says as you screech to a stop. "You think this is supposed to be fun?"

"Yes sir!"

The instructor scowls at you.

"I mean no sir!"

You hear the sound of diamond hooks above you. When you glance up, you see Dagma in a low crouch, leading the other cadets down the hill.

You've won!

"Congratulations cadet," the instructor says, giving you a mock salute. "Seems you've just earned yourself a promotion."

You can't wait to tell your family. They will be so proud. But you also realize this is only the beginning. You've only made it through basic training. Now the real work begins.

Seconds later, the other cadets are beside you. Some have their hands on their knees panting from exertion.

"Okay cadets, line up," the instructor says. "I'm pleased

you've all made it down without incident. I want you to meet your new troop leader."

The instructor waves you forward. You move off the line and come to stand by his side.

"Leaders are only as good as their troop," the instructor says to the assembled cadets. "If you don't work as a team out there on the slopes, none of you will survive a season. You all have strengths and weaknesses. The strongest of you isn't the fastest. The best in navigation isn't the best in communications. You all have a vital part to play in the Slider Corps. Our communities depend on you working together to keep them safe."

The instructor turns to you. It is time to dismiss your troop.

"Right you lot," you say. "Head back to the pod and get ready for our first patrol tomorrow morning at dawn."

As you are about to move off, the instructor places his hand on your shoulder. "Wait," he says. "We have some things to discuss."

As the other cadets enter a narrow portal cut into the black rock, you wonder what the instructor has to tell you.

Once the last cadet has disappeared he turns and gives you a serious look. "You know they look up to you," he says.

Do they really? You know Dagma doesn't. She just sees you as competition, as an obstacle to her rising through the ranks. How is she going to react to your promotion? Will she follow you when the going gets tough, or will she undermine your every move?

"Not all of them sir," you reply.

The instructor raises one eyebrow and scowls. "I know you and Dagma have had your differences, but she's got a lot of skill and determination. You'd do well to give her some respect and see if you can utilize her strengths."

"Yes sir."

"Now it's your choice, but you need to select one of the cadets to be second in charge. Do you know who you'd like?"

It is time for you to make an important decision. Do you:

Choose Dagma to be your second in charge because of her strength? **P20**

Or

Choose Gagnon as your second in charge because you like him better and he is a good navigator? **P24**

You have decided to follow Dagma and the others.

You see the pinnacles ahead, but realize you are moving too fast to make the turn into the chute. You have no option but to join the other cadets in their crazy slide down the main route.

Dagma is out in the lead due to her strong start, but her size is also creating more wind resistance and you know that if you optimize your stance you can gain some ground on her.

You bend your knees a little more and twist your torso so that you are as thin to the wind as possible. Your elbows are tucked tight to your sides and your guide stick trails behind you, just a fraction off the ground, ready to hook when you need to slow down.

A cadet to your right is trying to snag Dagma's harness with his stick and pull past her, but every time he reaches forward, either the wind catches him and slows him down, or Dagma bats his stick away with her own.

The slope is faster than you'd imagined. You've picked up so much speed you wonder if you'll be able to keep your feet once you hit the more uneven terrain below.

Some of the cadets have already started dragging their hooks, trying to slow themselves down before they sweep around a banked turn and enter a section of the course known as "the jumps".

Although this part of the mountain is not as steep as the slope higher up, it has a series of rounded humps to negotiate. Hit a hump too fast and you lose your balance. Get your timing wrong and you land on the uphill slope of the next hump and twist a knee or an ankle.

Everyone is moving too fast. The first jump is coming up sooner than expected. All around you the screech of hooks is deafening as the other cadets desperately try to slow down. Even Dagma is leaning hard on her hook, trying to reduce speed, before hitting the first jump.

This is your chance.

Rather than dropping your hook, you twist your lower body so that both feet are side by side and the lock-bar between your boots is side-on to the slope, rather than the traditional stance of one foot in front of the other. You bend your knees and get ready to spring up. Now it's just a matter of timing.

Your knees are forced to your chest when you hit the front of the hump. A split second later, as you near its crest, you spring up with all your strength.

The ground falls away as you soar through the air. "Woot, woot!" you yell. "I'm flying!

While holding your guide stick at arm's length in front of your chest, you swivel your lower body back around so your front foot is pointing straight down the hill again. Then you bend your knees a little and get ready for impact.

You've done it! When you make contact with the ground, it is on the downward side of the third jump, having cleared the second one altogether. You force you legs upwards and spring off the crest of the fourth jump and land on the downward side of the last jump with a satisfying swish of boots on rock. You tuck back into your arrow stance and gain even more speed as you race to the finish.

You can't believe how fast you are moving. This is so much faster than on the simulator. The wind is howling. Wow, what a feeling!

You see the finishing flag less than a quarter of a mile ahead. A quick glance back up the hill and you know you've won. The others are well back. One cadet has fallen and is sliding on his backside trying to regain his feet. Dagma is the best of the others, with Gagnon close behind.

You flash across the finish, rise from your crouch and drop your hook, forcing it down hard onto the shiny black surface. You screech to a halt next to an instructor.

"What are you smiling about cadet?" the instructor says. "You think this is supposed to be fun?"

"Yes sir!"

The instructor scowls.

"Well it is sir!"

The instructor's eyes soften as he suppresses a grin. "If you say so, cadet."

You hear the screech of hooks behind you as the others finish. Dagma bangs the ground with her stick in frustration.

"Congratulations," the instructor says, giving you a mock salute. "It seems you've just earned yourself a promotion."

You can't wait to tell your family. They will be so proud. But you also realize this is only the beginning. You've only made it through basic training. Now the real challenge begins.

"Okay line up cadets," the instructor says.

They shuffle into line, breathing hard.

"I'm please you've all made it down without incident. I want you to meet your new troop leader."

The instructor waves you forward. You push your shoulders back and stand by his side.

"Leaders are only as good as the troops they lead," the instructor says. "If you cadets don't work as a team out there on the slopes, none of you will survive a season.

The instructor taps his guide stick on the ground. "Right, head back to your pod and get ready for your first patrol tomorrow morning at dawn."

As you are about to move off, the instructor places his hand on your shoulder. "Wait," he says. "We have a few things to discuss."

You watch as the other cadets enter a portal that has been cut into the sheer black wall and head back towards their accommodation area. You wonder what the instructor has to tell you.

Once the others have gone, the instructor turns and looks into your eyes. "They look up to you," he says.

"Not all of them, sir," you reply.

The instructor raises one eyebrow. "I know you and Dagma have had your differences, but she's got a lot of skill and determination. You'd do well to give her some respect and see if you can utilize her strengths rather than concentrating on her weaknesses."

"Yes sir."

"Now it's your choice, but you need to select one of the cadets to be second in charge. Do you know who you'd like that to be?"

It is time for you to make an important decision. Do you:

Choose Dagma to be your second in charge because of her strength and skills? **P20**

Or

Choose Gagnon as your second in charge because you like him better and he is a better navigator? **P24**

You have chosen Dagma to be second in charge.

After thinking over what your instructor has said, you realize that you need to find a way to work with Dagma if your troop is going to become a cohesive unit. The sooner you can forget your differences, the better off everyone will be.

"Well?" the instructor says. "Who's it to be?"

You straighten your shoulders. "Dagma will make a good second, sir. The others will follow her without question if I am injured."

"Dagma it is then," the instructor says. "Now get back to your troop. You leave for the Pillars of Haramon at first light."

As you walk through the portal and down the corridor towards the accommodation pods, you take in the significance of what the instructor has just said. The Pillars of Haramon are an advanced base an 80-mile slide from the training ground. You've heard stories and seen pictures of these towering, fortified columns of black glass ever since you were a child. You remember the history lessons you've had about the brave miners who first discovered these diamond-packed volcanic pipes that rise nearly a thousand feet from the shining slopes below, and of the legendary sliders who have protected the outpost over the years.

These days the twin towers of rock are honeycombed with tunnels and chambers and form one of the Highland's strongest and most beautiful fortified positions. Mining still takes place deep beneath the pinnacles, but the above-ground pipes were cleaned out many years ago and now form sleeping, hydro, and defense pods.

As you walk along the corridor, you look up at the ceiling. Circular shafts have been bored to bring light down from the surface. Halfway along the first corridor a junction splits four ways. You turn right and follow the eastern access towards pod 6.

You still can't believe you're going to the Pillars of Haramon. You remember hearing stories about the battles fought against the Lowlanders who have tried to capture them and the rich source of blue diamonds they contain. But generations of Lowlanders have been repelled by the Highland Slider Corps. Many songs have been written about their bravery.

For years now the Lowlanders have been quiet, building up their forces and growing stronger. Everyone knows it is only a matter of time before they attempt another invasion. When that happens, it will be up to you, your troop, and others of the Highland Slider Corps to make sure they don't succeed.

The thought of war does not thrill you. Nobody really wins a war. Even the winning side loses people that can never be replaced. After a few more twists down the tunnels you reach Pod 6E.

The pod has curved walls with a series of notches cut into it. Each notch contains a cubicle complete with bunk and storage space for the cadet's personal effects. In the center there is a seating area with a table, large enough to accommodate the 30 person troop.

"Congratulations," Gagnon says as you enter. "That was a brave move you pulled out there."

"Lucky," Dagma says from the end of the table. "You could have been sliced and diced trying a stunt like that. Was it really worth the risk?"

You turn towards Dagma. "Luck's got nothing to do with it. It was a calculated risk I'll admit, but I've been practicing the move on the simulator."

"So who have you chosen for your second?" Dagma says. "Your friend Gagnon, I suppose."

The troop looks at you expectantly. Twenty-nine sets of eyes are upon you. This is your first act of command. Will they understand?

"I've chosen you, Dagma. You're the strongest across a range of skills. If we can work together I'm sure our troop will be the best to graduate this year. Gagnon will be our advanced scout, because he is our best navigator."

When you look around, you see heads nodding. Gagnon seems happy with his role. The tight muscles in Dagma's face have relaxed a little. You hope it is a sign of her becoming more cooperative.

"Now, hit your bunks," you say. "We leave for the Pillars of Haramon at first light."

This last statement has the troop buzzing. Whispers and comments pass between its members. They too have heard the legends.

"Dagma and Gagnon, would you please come into my

cubicle. We need to plan for tomorrow."

Gagnon grabs a map from a drawer in the table and follows Dagma. Once inside, he unfolds the map and sticks it to the wall of your cubicle.

"There are two possible routes to the Pillars," Gagnon says. "Do you want fast or safe?"

After a quick look at the routes, you turn to Dagma. "What do you think?"

"If it was just us three I'd say fast," she says. "But there is always a chance of rain and with a troop of newbies I think we should go for safe. The last thing we need is an accident on our first day out."

Both options have advantages. Fast means you'll spend less time exposed to the elements, which is a good thing, but the safe route will be easier for those with less skill.

It is time for you to make your next decision. Do you:

Choose the slower, easier route to the Pillars of Haramon? **P29**

Or

Chose the fast route and spend less time on the slopes in case of rain? **P39**

You have chosen Gagnon to be second in charge.

You've decided to choose Gagnon to be your second in command because you know he won't undermine your authority. He is also the troop's best navigator which is one of the most important jobs a slider can have.

Many sliders have come to grief because of a simple mistake in navigation. Take the wrong valley and you can end up going over a bluff or into a crevasse, especially in flat light, when the ground's contours are hard to see and cracks in the surface are hidden in shadow.

Sliders navigate by triangulation. The navigator takes sightings from at least three prominent features with a handheld compass. Mountaintops, bluffs, or pinnacles work best. The navigator then transfers these bearings onto the map. Somewhere on the map, these three lines will intersect to form a triangle. Your location will be somewhere inside that triangle.

The more accurate a cadet is when they map out the compass bearings, the smaller that triangle will be. Some cadets are sloppy and always end up with large triangles, while others, like Gagnon, have tiny triangles that show a high level of accuracy.

"Well," the instructor says. "Who's it to be?"

You straighten your shoulders. "Gagnon will make a good second, sir," you say, hoping you've made the right choice. "I think even Dagma will follow his orders without question if I am injured."

"Gagnon it is then," he says. "Now get back to your troop. You leave for the Pillars of Haramon at first light."

As you walk through the portal towards the accommodation pods, you take in the significance of what the instructor has just said.

The Pillars of Haramon is an advanced lookout some eighty miles from the training ground. You've heard stories and seen pictures of these towering pinnacles ever since you were a child. You remember the history lessons you learned at school about the miners who first discovered these diamond packed volcanic pipes rising a thousand feet from the shimmering slopes below and of the legendary sliders who have protected them.

They are honeycombed with tunnels and chambers. These form one of the Highlands strongest and most unusual outposts. Mining still takes place deep underground beneath the Pillars, and many diamonds are still being uncovered, but above-ground the diamonds were cleared out years ago.

Your footsteps echo. Initially the tunnel is lit by light penetrating in from the portal by reflecting off the mirror black surface of the walls. Deeper inside, circular shafts bored into the roof, bring light down from the surface. Your unit's pod is 6-East. Halfway along the first corridor a junction splits four ways. You turn right and follow the eastern access.

You remember hearing stories about the battles fought against the Lowlanders who tried to capture the Pillars and the rich source of blue diamonds they contain. Generations of Lowlanders have been repelled by the Highland Slider Corps and many songs have been written about their bravery.

For years now the Lowlanders have been quiet, building up their forces and growing stronger. It is only a matter of time before they invade again. When that happens, it will be up to you, your troop, and others of the Highland Slider Corps to make sure they don't succeed.

Pod 6E has curved walls. A series of notches are cut into the rock. Each recess contains a bunk and a shelf for storing personal effects. In the center of the pod a table, long enough to accommodate the whole troop takes pride of place.

"Congratulations," Gagnon says as you enter. "That was a brave move you pulled out there."

"Lucky," Dagma says from the end of the table. "You could have been sliced and diced trying a stunt like that. Was it really worth the risk?"

You turn towards Dagma. "It was a calculated risk I'll admit, but I've been practicing on the simulator more than most. The odds were in my favor."

"So who have you chosen for your second?" Dagma says. "Your friend Gagnon, I suppose."

The troop looks at you expectantly. There is a hum of voices.

"Yes, I've chosen Gagnon. You might be the strongest across a range of skills but with your attitude I'm not sure we can work together."

"But…" Dagma is stunned. It is obvious that she thought she'd win the downhill race, and now she's not even going to be second.

"But I want you to prove me wrong, so I'm going to make you advance scout. Your strength and sliding talent will give us a real advantage if we met Lowlanders. I'm sure if we work together, our troop can be the best to graduate this year."

When you look around, you see heads nodding. Gagnon seems happy with his role. Even the normally strained muscles in Dagma's face have relaxed a little. You've helped her save face by giving her an important role. Perhaps this new responsibility will make her more cooperative.

"Now, get some sleep," you say. "We leave for the Pillars of Haramon at first light."

This last statement has the troop buzzing. Whispers and comments pass between cadets. They too have heard the legends.

"Dagma, Gagnon, come into my cubicle, we need to plan for tomorrow."

Gagnon grabs a map and brings it with him. Dagma follows you and once inside, leans casually against the wall of your cubicle.

"There are two possible routes to the Pillars," Gagnon says, pointing to the map. "Do you want fast or safe? We'll be exposed for a shorter length of time if we take the quicker route."

After studying the map, you look at Dagma. "What do

you think?"

"If it was just us three I'd say fast," she says. "But with 30 newbies, I think we should take the slower route. The last thing we need is an accident on our first patrol."

It is time for you to make your next important decision. Do you:

Choose the slower and easier route to the Pillars of Haramon? **P29**

Or

Choose the faster route and spend less time of the slopes in case of rain. **P39**

You have chosen the slower, easier route to the Pillars of Haramon.

While the cadets sleep, you've been up studying the map. On it Gagnon has marked his suggested route to the Pillars of Haramon. For most of the trip you will traverse the upper slopes on one of the wider, main tracks. But you also want to become familiar with alternative routes in case a change of plan is required.

It's just as well you decided to take the slow route to the Pillars. Moments ago you received orders from Slider Command to take a class of mining students with you.

This seems unusual. You're only cadets yourselves. Why would your superiors give you such a responsibility? Traversing the high tracks will be dangerous enough without having to babysit a bunch of miners on your first patrol.

Even though all Highland children are given needle-boots as soon as they are old enough to toddle, and quickly become familiar with moving about on slippery ground, no sane Highlander would venture far from home without slider guides.

Escorting a group of mining students is a big job, especially when there's a possibility of rain. Even the best quality needle boots will lose over fifty percent of their grip on black glass if the surface becomes damp.

Because of their high cost, only members of the Slider Corps are issued with guide sticks, fitted with best-quality diamond hooks and premium tyranium crystals.

Mining students, traders and ordinary citizens are dependent on guides to move on even the simplest of routes between the communities, mines and hydroponic chambers dotted around the Black Slopes.

Your instructors have taught you all about guiding. They've taught you that having a plan-B is advisable. Now that your troop is escorting miners, you want a plan-C as well.

When the wake-up buzzer sounds, the peace and quiet is broken. The cadets bound out of their bunks and dress quickly. They sort their equipment, pack their backpacks and sit at the breakfast table with a bubbling nervousness.

You feel a few moon moths fluttering in your stomach too, but you are determined to keep your nervousness in check for the sake of your troop.

Gagnon looks over your shoulder at the map. "Check, check and double check, aye?"

You see the hint of a smile on his face. He seems as calm as ever.

"I like the route you've planned," you tell him, "but it never hurts to have options."

"The higher we stay, the more options we have. There is nothing worse than being caught on low ground."

"Slider rule number one," the two of you say in unison. "Altitude is advantage."

As every slider knows, it's hard to slide when you're already at the bottom.

Gagnon points to the map. "Once we get past Mount

Tyron we can follow Long Gully all the way to the Pillars. It's only a 1 in 30 gradient so it should provide a gentle ride for our passengers."

After making a few more notes, you join the other cadets. Most are eating their hydro with gusto, knowing that this will be the last fresh food they see for a while.

You help yourself to a large plate of the succulent greens and pour yourself a cup of steaming broth.

When Dagma comes to sit beside you, you secretly smile. Maybe your plan to include her is working.

"A lovely day for babysitting miners," she grumps.

You can understand why Dagma isn't thrilled, but you want the trip to start on a positive note. Negativity can easily ruin morale.

"I can't wait to see the Pillars," you say loudly. Around you, other members of your troop smile and nod. Your tactic worked.

Dagma shrugs and shovels another large spoonful of hydro into her mouth. She's a big unit, and it takes a bit of feeding to keep her energy levels up.

Then she looks up from her plate. "Couldn't the miners use their whizzo anchor bolt launchers and zippers to make their own way?"

"No," you say. "They're only students. Besides, it's way too dangerous with overloaded sledges. None of them would make it."

Dagma grunts and shovels more hydro.

Once you've finished eating, you stand and tap your cup

on the table. The rest of the cadets stop talking and look at you expectantly.

"You've all probably heard by now that we're escorting mining students today. We'll be leaving soon, so let's get this pod ready for departure. I'll see you at the bottom of the tow in fifteen minutes. Remember, we're professionals so act like it. Let's make the Slider Corps proud and the miners welcome."

The sound of scraping boots and excited voices echo off the pod's walls as cadets finish packing and tidy up their cubicles.

You put on your utility belt and adjust the strap on your backpack. Then you grab your newly acquired guide stick and make your way along the corridor back towards the portal. The walls of the corridor are as dark as your mood. Responsibility is a burden, but you know once you get used to it, it will be rewarding.

Outside the air is crisp and still. The sky is without any hint of cloud.

An instructor is waiting for you at the bottom of the first tow. Beside him stands a group of ten mining students, each with their own sledge loaded high with equipment. Once your troop has assembled, the instructor clears his throat and everyone goes silent.

"I know some of you are wondering why Slider Command has decided to give a group of cadets the responsibility of getting these mining students to the Pillars of Haramon," the instructor says as he looks out over those gathered before him. "It's certainly not something we planned on. But yesterday, one of our advanced units spotted a large number of Lowlanders camped in the northern foothills. It's estimated they outnumber the Highland Slider Corps by three to one. They also have some unusual equipment hidden under tarpaulins."

The cadet standing next to you gulps in the deathly silence.

"The Highland Slider Corps are now on high alert. All available personnel are moving into defensive positions. All leave has been cancelled and any further cadet training has been suspended."

The officer's expression is serious. "We all knew this day was coming."

The instructor sweeps his arm, indicating everyone before him. "Some of you standing here are sliders and some of you are miners, but remember first and foremost, you are Highlanders."

You look along your troop. Dagma's face is tight, her lips pressed together. One or two cadets look about ready to pee themselves.

"The Pillars of Haramon give us control of the upper slopes," the officer continues. "If the Lowlanders can't get up the mountain, they are below us and will remain vulnerable. We need your help if we are to keep the Highlands safe for our families. So, are you with me Highlanders?"

"Yes sir!" both the sliders and miners shout.

You step forward and salute the instructor. "Slider Troop 6E is ready for departure sir."

"Off you go then. Be careful, we need this equipment delivered safely."

You feel a wave of nervousness wash over you, but you are determined to do your family and the Slider Corps proud. "Yes sir," you say, straightening your back. "We'll get there or die trying sir."

"Just get there cadet. You are not allowed to die today. That is an order."

"Yes sir," you say. "No dying today, sir."

You look over your troop. "Right, three cadets per sledge, two front, and one back. Miners, double-check that your loads are secure and climb aboard."

The sliders form themselves into groups and attach their harnesses to the sledges. After checking their loads, the miners climb up and strap themselves on.

Pulling the sledges, the sliders shuffle towards the towline. The two front sliders stand opposite each other, one on either side of the humming cable. The slider at the back gets ready to act as brake if required.

The front sliders hook their tow clamps over the whirling cable and squeeze. As the clamps grip onto the cable, everyone accelerates up the hill.

You lead the last group. Dagma, because of her superior strength, is at the back of your sledge, ready to put on the brakes should your group become separated from the tow somehow.

When you reach the top of the first tow, you repeat the exercise up the next, and the next. Before you know it, the training ground is a faint speck in the distance.

At the top of the last tow, you stop briefly to enjoy the view. A range of glistening black peaks stretch off in the distance. You feel the cool wind that has blown in from the north and notice that faint wisps of cloud have appeared on the horizon.

You turn to your troop. "Right, Gagnon is our navigator, his group will take the lead. We've chosen the safest route to the Pillars of Haramon for a reason, so keep your speed down. Stay in control of your sledges at all times, and stay alert … Gagnon?"

Gagnon raises his arm and points to a tooth-shaped peak in the distance. "Our first waypoint is sixteen miles to the west, just beneath Mount Transor."

The cadets turn to look at the towering peak. Mount Transor is one of the many unclimbed mountains on Petron. Light reflects off its near-vertical face. The tops of even higher mountains can be seen through the haze further inland.

"Now that we're traversing," you tell your troop, "we'll travel with one cadet in front of the sledge to steer, and two behind for braking. I want the strongest sliders at the back and, if in doubt, slow down. Unlike our competition yesterday, this is not a race."

As the slider troop rearrange their order and refasten their harnesses, you do the same in preparation to leading your sledge. Once everyone is ready you wave your arm. "Okay move out!"

Gagnon leads. The track is about two sledge widths wide and slants ever so slightly downhill, which lets gravity do the work of moving the heavy sledges.

The sledge's metal runners slide easily over the ground. A fine coating of diamond dust on their outside edges keep the runners tracking in a straight line.

You look at the clouds and hope they stay away. Conditions can change rapidly in the mountains. Squalls often race in after picking up moisture from the lowlands. Troops have been surprised by rapidly moving fronts before. Your hand moves over your utility belt and checks that your tether and anchor bolt gun are in their usual places. One of the first things you learned as a cadet was how to fire an anchor into the rock and tether a sledge. The troop record for this procedure is six seconds, held by Gagnon.

After checking that your boots are firmly locked together, you point your front foot down the path and push with the needle end of your guide stick. Before long you are moving at a quick, walking pace, except you're not expending any energy. Gravity is doing all the work.

Those ahead of you are making easy work of the gentle terrain and everyone is starting to relax. The miners seem to be enjoying the ride. Dagma brings up the rear.

Just as you are thinking all is well, the lead slider in the group ahead of you takes a fall and loses grip on the surface. As soon as she hits the ground, the sledge behind her slews off course and slips perilously towards the edge of the track.

There is a screech of diamond hooks as the two cadets at the rear of the sledge lean down hard on their guide sticks. But one of the front runners has veered off the path onto steeper terrain.

As much as the cadets try to hold it, the weight of mining equipment is slowly pulling the sledge off the track.

"Get ready to brake, Dagma," you yell, giving a big push in an attempt get close enough to hook one of the brakemen on the sledge in front of you, in order to give them some extra stopping power.

You just hope that Dagma is as strong as you think she is, and that her technique will be enough to slow the runaway sledge.

"Ready when you are," Dagma calls out.

You can hear her boots scraping on the rock behind you.

Another big push and you've caught up to the group in front. You reach out with your stick and hook on to the backpack of a cadet in front of you.

"Brake, Dagma!" you yell.

As Dagma and the other cadet drop their hooks and dig them in, you feel the straps of your harness tighten.

Will this added pressure pull the guide stick from your hand? How could you lead your troop without it?

If you get tangled, both sledges could be in danger. As Dagma digs deeper, you hang on as tight as you can.

Your sweaty hands are beginning to slip. You are not sure if you can hold on.

"I'm losing it!"

It is time to make a quick decision. Do you:

Hang tighter onto to your guide stick and try to save the runaway sledge? **P47**

Or

Unhook your stick from the group in front and save your own group? **P55**

You have chosen the faster route to the Pillars of Haramon.

You're up well before the alarm buzzer to check the fast route that Gagnon has marked on the map. It is the most direct route way to the Pillars of Haramon but has some switchbacks and tricky sections to negotiate. One part you're particularly concern with is known as "Zigzag Drop".

As you pore over the map, a courier enters and hands you a bright green envelope.

The envelope contains orders to escort ten mining students to the Pillars, all the more reason to get there as quickly as possible.

The chance of rain is low, but you are convinced that moving quickly and exposing your troop and the miners to the elements for the least amount of time is the right thing to do.

Miners, traders and common people are reliant on linked transport — where sliders escort travelers on specially designed sledges — to get around the various tracks. There are many stories about unaccompanied travelers "going to the bottom".

You are thinking about the best way to organize your caravan when the silence is broken by the wake-up buzzer. Cadets bound out of their bunks and dress quickly. They sort their equipment, pack their backpacks and eat breakfast with a bubbling nervousness of quick sentences and subdued giggles.

Gagnon looks over your shoulder at the map "Fast is good, eh?

"I like the route you've planned," you tell him. "There are a few tricky sections, but we should be okay."

After making a few more notes, you join the others at the breakfast table. Most are eating like hungry morph rats, knowing it will be a while before they'll have a chance to eat something other than travel rations and the occasional cup of broth.

You fill a large plate and pour yourself some steaming broth. You're pleased when Dagma comes and sits beside you. Maybe your plan to include her is working.

"I hear we've got miners to escort," Dagma says.

"At least it will give us a chance to show off our skills."

Dagma shrugs and shovels a large spoonful of stringy hydro into her mouth. Green strands hang down to her chin. She noisily slurps them up. You turn your head in disgust.

You stand up and tap your cup on the table. The rest of the cadets stop talking and raise their eyes.

"You all probably know by now that we're escorting a group of mining students to the Pillars of Haramon. We'll be leaving soon, so let's get this pod squared away for departure. I'll see you at the bottom of the towline with your gear in fifteen minutes.

The sound of scraping boots and mumbled voices fill the pod as the cadets move to their cubicles and finish packing.

You put on your utility belt and adjust the straps of your

backpack. Then you grab your guide stick. It is your prize possession. You turn it up and check the tyranium crystal pad on its foot by running your thumb over the tightly compacted ultra-fine needles. They seem in good condition. At the other end of the six-foot-long handle is a two inch hook of pure blue. This diamond is the hardest material on the planet, it will dig into anything. It will slow you down when sliding on the slopes, and also act as a weapon if required.

Happy with your equipment, you make your way out of the pod and along the corridor back to the portal. Outside you find an instructor and ten mining students. One of the mining students is laughing and joking around. His high pitched squeal rings out over the assembly.

Unfortunately, the instructor is not in a mood for jokes. "If you're finished playing around, Piver, it's time to listen up."

Suddenly, it is so quiet that you can hear the distinctive screech of a red-beaked pango miles down the valley.

The instructor clears his throat. "Yesterday one of our scouts spotted a large number of Lowlanders gathered in the northern foothills. It's estimated they outnumber the Highland Slider Corps by three to one."

"Geebus!" you hear the funny little miner say as his face goes pale.

The instructor gives him a sharp look and continues. "The Highland Slider Corps are now on high alert. All leave has been cancelled."

Groups of miners and sliders are a buzz of conversation at this news.

The instructor holds up his hand, requesting silence. "Controlling the Pillars of Haramon gives us control of the Black Slopes. As long as we control the base and Haramon Pass at the head of Long Gully, the Lowlanders can't gain access to the pathways and reservoirs we have developed over the centuries. We need your help if we are to keep the Highlands free and safe for our families. Are you with me?"

"Yes sir!" the sliders and miners shout in unison.

You step forward and salute the instructor. "Slider Corps 6E is ready for departure sir."

"Off you go then. We need these miners and their equipment at the Pillars as quickly as possible."

A wave of nervousness floods over you, but you are determined to do your family and the Corps proud. You straighten your back. "Yes sir."

"Don't allow the Lowlanders to cut you off."

"Yes sir. We're going to take the fast route. With luck we'll avoid contact with any Lowland patrols that way."

"Luck's got nothing to do with it cadet. Just remember your training and everything will be fine."

You salute once more and then look over at your group. The miners' sledges are loaded to the max with equipment.

"Right sliders," you call out. "Two per sledge, one front and one back. The rest of you, keep an eye out for Lowlanders. Miners, climb aboard and strap in tight, this is going to be a quick trip."

As you watch, twenty cadets harness themselves up to the heavy sledges leaving ten cadets free for quick deployment should Lowlanders be spotted along the route. A mining student jumps aboard each sledge.

"Ready to tow," the front cadet on the first sledge says.

You nod and lift your arm. "On my mark, three, two, one… go!"

The leading cadet hooks the tow clamp attached to the front of his harness, over the whirling cable and squeezes its handles. As the clamp grips the cable, the slack is taken up in the cadet's harness and the sledge begins to move up the hill.

Your group brings up the rear. Once you reach the top of the first tow, everyone repeats the exercise up the next tow, and the next. Soon the training ground is a speck far below and you can see the curvature of the planet off in the distance.

At the top of the last tow you stop briefly to enjoy the view. Peak after shining black peak stretch off into the distance.

Pleased at the lack of cloud in sight, you turn to your troops. "Right, Gagnon is our navigator. He will take the lead for now. We've chosen the quick route for a reason, so keep moving. Our first waypoint is sixteen miles to the west near Mt Tyron."

You look towards the towering peak in the distance. Light glints off its reflective face as the sun tracks around to the west.

Once everyone is ready you wave your arm. "Okay, move out!"

Gagnon, unencumbered by a sledge, shoves off with a push of his stick. The line of sledges follow.

Most of the sledges are overloaded with extra gear from Command. This equipment is needed at the Pillars to defend against the impending Lowland attack. The cadets at the back of the sledges are constantly dragging their hooks to keep them from gaining too much momentum as they make their way along the narrow track traversing the across the slope.

You feel every bump and irregularity as you slide along. Occasionally you need to correct your balance. A quick tap of your stick on the ground is usually all that is required. But you must keep alert. Things on the upper slopes can change in an instant.

When you hear a series of high-pitched screeches, you look up and see a flock of pangos heading out to feed. Their formation creates a massive V in the sky. The bird's wings barely move as they soar on the thermals created by the hot air rising from the dark, heat-absorbing slopes below

Above the pangos, Petron's smallest moon glows a faint pink. A fuzzy ring around it circumference shows that there is moisture in the upper atmosphere.

Instinctively you pat your utility belt and feel the row of anchor bolts every slider carries in case of emergency. If you are caught in a sudden downpour you'll only have seconds to fire a charge into the slope and clip yourself on. If you are too slow, you'll be swept down the slope without any chance of stopping.

You point your front foot ever so slightly downhill and push with your guide stick. It doesn't take much to get moving on the slick rock. Before long, the troop is moving along at a running pace, except you're not expending any energy. Gravity is doing all the work.

This track is steeper than the usual transport tracks. Still, everyone seems to be coping with the gradient so far. The troop is making good speed and you start to relax.

Just as you are thinking all is well, you hear a shout. The cadet leading the front sledge has fallen.

You can see the brakeman struggling to stop.

When a steering runner slips off the main track onto the steeper slope below, the front of the sledge lurches and skews sharply downhill. Its speed increases in an instant.

"Abandon sledge!" the brakeman yells. "I can't hold it!"

The fallen cadet unclips her harness and kicks herself out of the heavy sledge's path. Then she spins onto her back and digs in her heel spurs. The miner hits the quick release on his waist strap, jumps off the sledge, and rolls onto his belly, digging the tip of his pick into the slope to stop his slide.

The brakeman unclips his harness and, pressing hard on his guide stick, comes screeching to a halt.

As the runaway sledge rockets down the hill, you hear gasps from your group. Thankfully its crew, although shaken, seems to be okay. The slider who first fell is up and has made her way to the miner who is hanging onto his pick for dear life. With a *pop* an anchor bolt is fired into the rock and the miner is secured. Another cadet throws down a cable and those below clip on and start working their way back up to the track where the rest of you wait anxiously.

"Geebus!" a familiar voice exclaims. "That was close!"

You realize how right the funny little miner is. It's time to reassess things. Maybe taking the fast route with a troop of untested cadets wasn't such a good idea after all. But then the extra time you've taken after the accident means you are behind schedule.

What do you do now? It is time to make an important decision. Do you:

Slow down and put more safety precautions in place? **P85**
Or

Carry on down to the Pillars and make best speed. **P102**

You have decided to hang on to your guide stick and try to save the runaway sledge.

At first the strain is so great you think your arms will be pulled from their sockets. Your muscles burn, but you grit your teeth and hang on. Then after a few seconds, the pressure eases. Dagma and her fellow cadet have managed to bring the uncontrolled slide to a halt.

Once you come to a complete stop, you unhook your stick from the harness of the cadet in front of you and exhale with relief. "Are you all alright?"

The cadet who had been steering the sledge is back on her feet and looking over the pile of equipment at you. "Thanks. I've got it now."

The two cadets at the rear of the runaway sledge are red-faced and panting from exertion.

"Thanks for that," one says.

The other cadet tries to put on a brave face. "Yeah thanks. We nearly went to the bottom that time."

Everyone knows exactly what he means when he says "the bottom". The bottom is not a place people come back from … well, not often, anyway.

You shake your head and try to get the ugly thought out of your head. "Okay, let's heave this sledge back onto the track and try it again."

As the cadets get to work, you can see they are still a little shaken from their close call … and so they should be.

Once the sledge is safely up and its load secured, it's time to move off again.

"Let's take it a little slower this time," you say.

Thankfully, for the rest of the morning your group slides on without incident. Gradually your nerves settle down and you relax once more.

For lunch you stop on a small plateau which provides enough flat ground for everyone to anchor their sledges. It is the junction where the west and eastbound tracks cross.

The cadets remove their harnesses and sit on the ground. It's been a long morning. Tired legs and backs need a break. Ration packs are broken open and burners are lit to heat broth.

Gagnon informs you that the troop has traveled just over seventeen miles and lost 3000 feet of altitude.

You do a quick mental calculation. That equates to thirty feet of forward progress for every foot of lost altitude, pretty good going for a group of rookies. "At this rate we'll reach our camp well before dewfall," you say to Gagnon.

Since the accident you've been moving slower, but you know that once you get to smoother slopes your troop will be able to make up some time.

Lunch lasts half an hour. You make a few adjustments to the teams, and give Gagnon a break from leading now that you've come off the face and have reached a wide valley that is almost impossible to get lost in.

Dagma is keen to lead so you put Gagnon with her team at the rear and send Dagma forward to lead the next section.

"Just remember, Dagma, we're not all as strong as you, so

keep your speed down."

Dagma gives you a curt nod and steps into the lead sledge's harness. "Don't worry, I know what I'm doing," she says. "Remember, I've done just as many hours as you have on the simulators."

You're still not sure about Dagma's attitude. She seems determined to prove to everyone how good she is despite what is best for the team. You suspect she still hasn't forgiven you for beating her in the race to become troop leader.

Before you have a chance to say "move out", Dagma is off, pushing with big strokes to get her sledge up to speed.

"Let's go," you say to the others. "Go at your own pace and don't worry if Dagma gets a bit of a lead on you. This is not a race."

The valley is nearly half a mile wide, mainly smooth and at the perfect angle for sliding. It stretches far into the distance. Steep hills crowd in on both sides. Occasionally a vertical pillar of black rock will rise up from the otherwise featureless landscape. These dormant volcanic pipes are a constant reminder of Petron's volcanic past.

The young miner on your sledge makes a comment about the possibility of blue diamonds being present in the pipes as you pass. His voice is filled with excitement and nervousness at the same time. You are happy to chat. It helps pass the time on this less demanding part of the journey, but after a while you start getting a sore throat from having to shout over the sound of the wind whistling around your visor as you whiz down the slope.

The planned stopping point for the night is a fortified tow-base near the bottom of this valley, almost ten miles away. Then tomorrow, you'll tow up to the top of a ridge where you'll find the track that will take you to Long Gully and then on to the Pillars of Haramon.

The tow-base has a maintenance crew of ten and a number of accommodation, defense and hydro pods bored into the solid rock. It will be a crowded night with the miners and their cargo, but even crowded accommodation is better than being out on the slopes after dewfall.

When you look down the valley you see that Dagma has pulled away from the rest of the troop. You shake your head and grumble under your breath. Why does she always need to prove herself like this?

You are about to send Gagnon off after her to tell her to slow down when your eyes are distracted by movement below and off to your left.

It takes a second to realize that what you've seen is a group of Lowlanders working their way up the left hand edge of the valley about half a mile away. The Lowlanders' dark uniforms are nearly invisible against the shimmering black rock.

Dagma has missed them. Unfortunately she is too far away for you to yell out a warning. You grab your scope and watch as the Lowland scouts raise their bows and prepare to fire at Dagma's group.

Luckily you've noticed the Lowlanders while you are still

well above them. Your troop's camouflage is even better than the Lowlanders'. Even the sledges are almost invisible with their shiny black covers.

The Lowlanders haven't seen you. They must think that Dagma's group is travelling solo. You have the advantage.

You raise your fist with one finger extended, the signal for a silent stop. The cadets slow the sledges by turning them side on to the slope rather than dragging their noisy hooks.

"Lead cadets prepare for attack," you whisper once you've pulled to a halt.

You unhook your harness and spin your backpack around so it rests against your chest to act as a shield. Then you unlock your boots so you have a full range of movement.

"V-formation," you order. "We'll send them to the bottom before they know what's hit them."

You and nine other sliders group together, sitting on your utility belts with packs to the front. Your guide sticks are tucked tight under your arms with the hook end forward and the crystal end resting on the ground ready to steer you one way or the other in an instant.

"On my count," you say quietly. "Three, two, one, push…"

Within seconds, your formation is sliding down the slope, each cadet tucked close, protecting the cadet beside them.

"Time to increase our speed and show these Lowlanders who owns the slopes," you shout over the whistling wind.

On the front of your pack, behind a thin protective plate,

is a small reservoir. You pull a lever and a fine stream of water shoots out onto the slope in front of you. After sliding through the damp patch, you feel the friction lessen and your troop accelerate like someone has fired a rocket launcher.

"Hard left, on my mark. Three, two, one, now!"

The cadets follow your order instinctively, forcing their guide sticks hard against the smooth rock and pushing your tightly-packed group to the left. You are bearing down on the Lowland scouts, sliding faster and faster.

A Lowlander looks up and sees you coming. He warns the others. They stop firing at Dagma and turn to face your group racing towards them.

"Sticks up!" you yell.

"Woot, woot!" your cadets yell.

The Lowlanders reload and fire. But your group is still accelerating and they misjudge their aim. Only one arrow strikes a member of your group and it is deflected by the cadet's armored backpack.

Your group is close now. The diamond spurs imbedded in the heel of your boots sparkle in the sunlight, ready to strike like fangs at the legs of the invaders.

When you collide with the Lowlanders, it is with such force that despite their protective armor, they fly off their feet and are propelled down the slope.

The impact has had the reverse affect on you and your cadets. It's brought you nearly to a halt.

"Hooks down!" you command.

The piercing screech of diamond digging into the black rock reminds you of the call of the wild pango as your cadets come to a stop. Their grim expressions have turned to elated smiles at having survived their first encounter with Lowlanders.

Down the valley to your right, Dagma has brought her sledge to a stop and is tending a cadet with an arrow sticking out of her leg.

The Lowlanders are off their feet and free sliding out of control. You watch their desperate attempts to stop before they run into something nasty. Then, as the terrain flattens out a little, the Lowlanders manage to bring their slide to a halt. Despite being bruised and battered they've survived, but they don't hang around. They quickly organize themselves and retreat further down the slope. Before long they are nothing but dots in the distance, scurrying home in defeat.

"Sliders one, Lowlanders nil," you say to your troop. "Well done. Now, I suppose we'd better slide over and see if we can help Dagma."

You signal the cadets who remained with the sledges further up the hill, to proceed with caution down the slope and then stand up, lock your boots together and start pushing your way towards Dagma.

The cadet hit by the arrow is in pain, but at least the arrow missed all the major arteries, nor has it hit bone. After disinfecting the wound and wrapping a bandage around the cadet's thigh, she has no problem standing. The wounded cadet is given a couple of yellow capsules, a combination pain killer and antibiotic, and helped to her feet.

"Let's get you on one of the sledges," you say. "You'll be fine in a day or two if you take it easy."

"It's only a scratch. I can slide," she says gritting her teeth. "The pain killers should kick in soon."

You shake your head. "You may be able to slide, but for now there's no need. Just rest until we get to the tow-base."

Finding Lowlanders along your intended route was unexpected. It also means you need to make a decision. Do you:

Carry on down the slope towards the tow-base in your current formation? **P102**

Or

Send some advanced scouts to test the route first? **P111**

You have decided to unhook from the sledge in front and save your own group.

The guide stick is being pulled from your grasp. You know that if you don't unhook from the group ahead you will lose it, or even worse, send the sledge you are leading tumbling down the steep hillside as well.

With a twist of your wrist you free yourself from the group in front. Will they be able to stop without your help?

You aren't sure, but it's up to them now. Both of the brakemen are desperately trying to stop the runaway sledge but seem to be fighting a losing battle. The miner on the sledge is panicking and looks ready to jump.

"Stay on the sledge!" you yell. But has he heard you? If he jumps now, you know he'll end up sliding out of control. You doubt his pick will be enough to stop him from slipping all the way to the bottom. At least on the sledge he's got a chance.

Then miraculously, the lead slider regains her feet and with a desperate drive of her guide stick manages to turn the nose of her sledge side-on to the slope. The sledge is still moving fast, but without gravity trying to drag it down the mountain, the momentum is reduced. The two cadets at the back renew their efforts and gradually the sledge slows.

You exhale loudly and wipe the sweat off your forehead.

"Phew, that was close," you mumble as you slip out of your harness and slide closer to where the runaway sledge has come to a stop. They are slightly below you and off the main track, but at least they are all in one piece. The miner is white-faced and trembling.

With some ropes and extra pulling power you and your cadets manage to get the runaway sledge back onto the main track. After 30 minutes your troop is back in formation and ready once again to move off.

You've had a lucky escape. Thankfully, for the rest of the morning everyone slides on without incident.

For lunch you stop on a small patch of flat ground which provides enough space for everyone to remove their harnesses and anchor their sledges. Most of the sliders sit to give their sore legs and backs a break. Ration packs are broken open and a small burner is fired up to heat broth.

Gagnon informs you that the troop has traveled just over seventeen miles. "And we've only lost 3000 feet of altitude. That's thirty feet of forward progress for every foot of lost altitude, pretty good going for a group of rookies."

"And despite the accident, we're making good time," you say to Gagnon, acknowledging his navigational and route planning skills. "At this rate we'll reach the tow-base an hour before dewfall."

After lunch, you decide to take the lead and give Gagnon a break. There isn't much navigation to do in this section because you'll be travelling down a broad valley.

The terrain on the right-hand side of the valley is undulating but smooth. The other side is a different matter. A major fault line has created a chaotic jumble of crevasses and ridges. Not the sort of place to want to take sledges anywhere near.

"Remember to keep well to the right," you tell the cadets as you push off with your stick. "We've still got a fair way to go. Let's try to keep things unexciting."

For the first fifteen miles everything goes without a hitch, but when you see movement up on the slope to your right, you order everyone to come to a halt.

You take out your scope and focus. It is a group of fifteen Lowland scouts, climbing up towards the ridge. How did they get past the lookouts at the tow-base? How are they managing to get a grip on the steep slope? Have the Lowlanders developed some new technology that allows them to move on the slick black glass? Maybe they've found a source of needle crystals.

"Can your catapult reach that far?" you ask Dagma.

Dagma pulls out her scope and points it at the group of Lowlanders. After making a few adjustments she lowers the instrument and looks at its dial. "It's reading just over half a mile. We'll need to get closer to have a chance of reaching them."

With the Lowlanders holding the high ground, their arrows will reach your group before your catapults can knock them off their perch. Sending your cadets any closer would be suicidal.

As you discuss the problem with Dagma, the miner riding on your sledge coughs. "Can I make a suggestion?" he says.

You nod. "As long as you do it quickly."

"I've got a cable launcher on my sledge," he says before

pointing up the slope towards a small pinnacle on a rise behind you. "If we fire a line up to that outcrop, you can use my heavy-duty zipper to gain some altitude."

You think about what the miner has said. "How many cadets will it hold?"

The miner thinks a bit. "Six or seven I would think. Will that be enough?"

"It should be."

Sliders always try to attack from above. All their tactics are based on having the advantage of altitude. Trying to dislodge the Lowlanders from below will almost certainly mean the loss of some of your cadets.

After a brief discussion with Dagma you turn to the miner. "Okay, break it out. Let's get it set up before the Lowlanders realize what we're up to."

The miner removes the cover off his sledge and grabs a long tubular piece of equipment. This is attached to a sturdy tripod.

After setting the launcher up, the miner looks through a scope on the top of the firing tube and adjusts dials and levers. Then he attaches a spool of ultrafine cable to the back of a sleek projectile with fins on its tail and fits it into the back of the tube.

"Ready to fire," the miner says.

You've decide to lead the attack yourself so you grab the miner's heavy-duty zipper and attach it to the front of your harness ready to clamp onto the towline as soon as it is secure. Five other cadets link up to you, one behind the other. You look at the miner. "On my count. Three, two, one, fire!"

The miner pulls the trigger and the projectile hisses towards the pillar. The reel of cable whirls out after it.

A puff of dust erupts from the pinnacle as the projectile buries itself deep into the rock.

"Ready to zip on my mark. Three, two, one!"

You squeeze the grip on the battery-powered zipper and next thing you know you and five cadets are rocketing up the side of the valley.

As you slide, you wonder if the Lowlanders have spotted you. Surely they've heard the launcher or have seen you, despite your uniforms blending into the dark rock of the slope.

When you reach the top of the tow the zipper cuts out. The six of you look towards the Lowlanders. They are below you now, but not by much.

"Okay, get ready to traverse," you tell your cadets. "We need to get closer before they have time to get any higher. Dagma, let us know when you're within catapult range."

The other cadets follow as you push off with your stick. The swish of your boots sliding across the smooth rock sounds like compressed air escaping from a hydro growing chamber. You try to keep as high as possible as you traverse across the hillside.

It isn't long before Dagma signals a halt. "I think I can reach them from here."

She removes a Y-shaped piece of metal and strong

synthetic tube from the top of her backpack along with a handful of water bullets. Each bullet is about the size of a pango egg and has a rigid shell designed to break on impact.

"Aim well above them," you say to Dagma.

Dagma slips a water bullet into the catapult's pouch and stretches the tubing back with all her strength. With a *zing* the bullet arcs off into the sky and splats on the uphill side of the Lowlanders.

The water, now released from its container, has nowhere to go but down.

You notice the first of the Lowlanders slip slightly as the first trickle runs under his feet. When Dagma's second bomb hits the slope they are all scrambling for anchor points.

Now that the Lowlanders' attentions are fully focused on staying attached to the slope, you can move closer. There is no way any of them are going to let go of their anchor points long enough to fire an arrow.

"Forward," you order.

You push off and slide closer to the Lowlanders' position. When you feel all the cadets will be able to reach the Lowlanders with their catapults, you motion them to stop.

"Load up hard shot," you say, grabbing your catapult and some lumps of stone from a side pouch of your backpack. "Let send these invaders to the bottom."

The Lowlanders are in trouble now. If they let go of their anchor points they will plummet down the hillside. If they don't, they will be pounded by hard-shot.

The Lowlanders' only choice is to rappel down on whatever cables they have and retreat with all haste. Even then it is unlikely that all of them will get away without injury. You see one of their scouts frantically untangling a cable and attaching it to an anchor point he's quickly fixed to the rock.

Just as he's about to clip on, he's knocked off his feet. He lurches for the cable as he falls, but misses it by a hand's width.

"That's one off," Dagma cries with glee. "Now let's get the rest of them!"

The cadets are all firing now. Hard shot is peppering the remaining Lowlanders. Desperately they push each other aside in their attempt to be first down the cable.

When another Lowlander slips and starts sliding towards the bottom, a cheer goes up.

Dagma fires more water bullets to keep the slope as slick as possible. The remaining cadets keep the hard shot flying. The Lowlanders are taking a beating.

Finally, the remaining Lowlanders manage to clip on and abseil down the cable at breakneck speed.

A mile or so down the valley the two Lowlanders who were knocked off have managed to stop and are regrouping. You peer through your scope and see them tending to their scrapes and bruises. Once the remaining Lowlanders have made it to the valley floor, two of them pull out their bows.

"After them," you say. "V-formation on my mark!"

Your cadets stow their catapults and unlock their boots.

They reverse their backpacks, so they cover their chest and act as a shield, and point the hook end of their guide sticks to the front. The cadets sit on their utility belts in a V formation and lock arms, ready for a super-fast downhill slide.

"On my mark … three, two, one, go!" you yell.

When the Lowlanders see your flying wedge coming down the hill at them, they realize the hopelessness of their situation, drop their bows and flee.

"Hard right on my mark!"

You and your cadets push right with your sticks.

"Again!" you yell.

As one, your cadets stab the ground with the needle end of their sticks, aiming themselves at the Lowlanders.

"Line formation! Boots up!"

In seconds, what was a V-formation is a line spread across the slopes. Cadets have their sticks up like lances and their diamond studded heels raised, ready to knock the Lowlanders off the mountain.

The Lowlanders' eyes are huge. They have seen all they need to. With a yelp of panic they fling themselves down the hillside. By the time your troops hit the valley floor they are scurrying off toward their unlucky comrades further down the mountain.

"Hooks down!" you order.

You swivel your stick around and dig its hook into the slope behind you. You don't need your eyes to tell the other cadets are following suit. The screech of diamond on black glass is unmistakable.

Your cadets have all stopped within a few yards of each other.

"Well they won't be back for a while," Dagma says with a grin.

You stand and signal the cadets further up the valley to bring the sledges down. Then you look at the young Highlanders around you.

"Stop grinning, cadets! Do you think this is supposed to be fun?"

Your cadets hesitate a moment.

Then you burst out laughing. "Of course it is! Now let's give those Lowlanders a slider farewell!"

"Woot, Woot!" the cadets yell. "Woot, Woot, Woot!"

By the time your caravan is reorganized, the Lowlanders have disappeared and you have the valley to yourselves again. It's time to proceed towards your destination. You cross your fingers and hope for an uneventful afternoon.

But after sliding for less than an hour a miner, who's been looking through his scope, yells "Stop! There's something strange going on."

Once again you order the troop to a halt and pull out your scope.

Then you see what the miner is pointing at. There is an eerie light coming from a split in the side of a small rocky outcrop about 200 yards up the slope to your left.

"What's that glow?" you ask the miner. "Is it light reflecting off blue diamonds, do you think?"

At the mention of diamonds, everyone is scrabbling for their scopes.

The miner shakes his head. "I don't think so. It could be tyranium crystals, but it would have to be a pretty big deposit to glow so brightly."

Whatever it is, it isn't normal. Could it be a Lowland trap? You look up at the sky and calculate the time left before dewfall. There is just enough time to investigate, but you will be cutting it fine.

It is time to make a decision. Do you:

Go investigate what is causing the blue light? **P65**

Or

Keep going and forget about the blue light? **P71**

You have decided to go investigate what is causing the blue light.

"Get a cable launcher set up," you tell a couple of miners. "Dagma, you and I will investigate. Gagnon, stay here with the rest of the troop."

"Shall we get our catapults ready?" Gagnon asks. "Just in case?"

"Good idea. But be ready to take off in a hurry if something happens or Dagma and I get captured."

There is a buzz of voices as you and Dagma adjust your harnesses in preparation for a quick ride up to the outcrop.

Within minutes the two of you are zipping towards the eerie glow. As you climb, you see moon moths flitting about.

"Those moths are acting strangely," Dagma says.

The higher you climb the more moths you see. They are congregating around the crack in the rock.

"Moths are always attracted to the light," you say.

Dagma shakes her head. "But look at the patterns they are forming. They're like mini tornadoes."

Dagma is right. The moths are swirling funnels of iridescent blue, the bottom tip of which points down into the crack.

The zipper cuts out when you and Dagma reach the end of the cable. You unclip and slide your way over to the hole in the rock. As usual, Dagma rushes ahead.

Never have you seen so many moon moths in one place.

"I can squeeze through," Dagma says.

Before you can say "wait" she's disappeared into the opening.

Then you hear her laughing.

Of all the cadets in your troop, Dagma is the least jovial. Normally to get her laughing, someone has to break a leg or step in pango poo.

It's hard to believe it's actually her cackling away.

At the opening, you push your head through the swarm of swirling moths and look in. As soon as you do, you realize the crack is actually the opening to a large cave that extends quite some distance into the hillside. Due to the many moon moths, it is almost as bright inside as it is outside.

You hear laughter again. This time it's above you. You look up and see Dagma and a hundred or more moon moths. They have picked her up and are swooping around the cave with her dangling in mid air. Others are fluttering around, tickling her under the chin and spraying a fine mist into her face.

Dagma is laughing and woot-wooting like she's been drinking fermented fruit broth.

"Isn't this great?" Dagma yells. "Look I'm flying!"

Dagma is flying all right. What are those moths spraying into her face?

It isn't long before you find out. You were so busy watching Dagma swooping around that you didn't feel a bunch of moths grab onto the fabric of your uniform and lift you off your feet.

When you open your mouth in surprise, moths spray a slightly sweet mist into your mouth.

Instantly you relax. It's as if flying is the most natural thing in the world.

The moon moths are taking you deeper and deeper into the cave.

"Where are we going?" you ask Dagma.

"I don't know, but I don't care. This is so much fun!"

It isn't until you hear a familiar scurrying, and the gnashing of teeth that you start to worry.

"I hear morph rats," you tell Dagma.

"Me too. Woot woot! Here ratty, ratty."

Is this the Dagma you know? What has got into her? Here ratty ratty? Is she nuts?

Then you see where the moon moths are taking you. This is their breeding chamber. Hundreds of slender transparent tubes hang from the roof of the cave. Inside each tube you can see a dozen or so moth larva. On the floor of the cave below the tubes, morph rats are piling up on top of each other in an attempt to reach the baby moths.

"I think they want us to save their babies," Dagma says. "Look!"

You turn to where Dagma is pointing and see fifty or so moon moths picking up morph rats and dropping them into a pit at one side of the cave, but more rats are entering the cave than the moths can't deal with.

"Have you got a screecher?" you ask Dagma.

She reaches for her utility belt. "Just the one."

"Let it rip," you say. "We'll just have to plug our ears."

You pull two plugs from your utility belt and stuff one in each ear, then nod to Dagma.

Even with the earplugs, the screecher is loud. But loud for you is unbearable for the morph rats. It's only seconds before they start rushing from the chamber like their lives depend on it.

As you hover above, it's like watching water run down a plughole as the rats swirl around and dive into the pit to escape the sound of the screecher. In less than a minute, all that remains is the smell of fart.

A swarm of moths flutter about your face, ticking you under the chin and around your ears. Both you and Dagma are laughing now.

"We'd better get going," you tell Dagma. Dewfall isn't far away.

Dagma gives you a big smile. "These moths will hatch out in the next day or two. It would be a pity if the rats came back and ate them all. Maybe I should stay and protect them?"

You think about what Dagma has said. It must be the mist, Dagma usually only worries about herself. A couple days with the moths would probably do her good.

"Maybe I could train them to fly me places?" Dagma says. "Wouldn't that be good for the Slider Corps?"

She's right. Trained moths would be an amazing advantage. Imagine swooping over the slippery slopes without being reliant on needle boots and guide sticks.

"Okay, come back down to the sledges and get what you need. I'm sure there are a few extra screechers around somewhere. While you're here, try to find the spot where the rats are getting in and plug up the hole. Then the moths will be okay next year."

Dagma nods enthusiastically. "I think I saw some tyranium crystals when the moths were flying me around too. I'll try to collect them and bring them down when I come back to the Pillars of Haramon."

Ten minutes later, Dagma is heading back up to the chamber, armed with four screechers and a pack full of supplies. She still has a big smile on her face, possibly from the moth mist, or maybe it's just that for the first time in her life she's actually let herself have some fun.

(some years later)

"And did Dagma get back to the Pillars of Haramon okay Grandee?"

You adjust your grandchild on your knee and ruffle their hair.

"She sure did. Not only did she come back, she brought some pet moths with her. She was always happy after that and used to tell the funniest jokes ever. She's the reason Highlanders say, "What a dag", when something's funny."

"Geebus! Really? They named a word after her?"

"They sure did. Maybe one day we'll slide over and pay her a visit."

Well done. You've reached the end of this part of the story, but have you tried all the different endings? You now have another decision to make. Do you:

Go back to the very beginning and try another path? **P1**

Or

Go to the list of choices and start reading from another part of the story? **P216**

You have decided to keep going and forget about the blue light.

As interesting as the light is, getting to the Pillars of Haramon before dewfall is more important. You can always come back when you've got more time and less responsibility.

After getting everyone lined up and ready to move out again, you have a feeling in your gut that there might be more Lowlanders about.

"Dagma," you say. "It might be a good idea if you to take the lead for a while. I'd rather we have our best and strongest cadets at the front.

Dagma loves being out in front. She moves forward.

"On my mark, two, one…" Dagma yells, wasting no time in pushing off.

The only thing Dagma loves more than being in front is going fast. Everyone in the troop is fully concentrating on the sledge in front just to keep up with her breakneck pace.

It's not until you notice your shadow is in front of you, rather than on your left where it should be, that you realize Dagma, in her haste, has taken a wrong turn and led you down a side valley.

"Stop!" you yell out. "You're going the wrong way!"

You pull out a map, and spread it out on top of the sledge's cover.

Gagnon slides over to have a look too.

You point to an area on the map that is littered with

crevasses. It is directly between you and your destination.

"Pango poo!" Gagnon says, "I should have been paying more attention. Now we've got to climb all the way back up to where we missed the turn, or find a way through the crevasse field."

You pull out your scope and focus on the crevasses.

"They don't look too bad," you say to Gagnon. "Maybe we should try to cut across rather than go all the way back up. We'll never make it to safety before dewfall if we do that."

"The field isn't properly mapped," Gagnon say. "But, if we take it slow…"

You look at the sun sinking towards the horizon. It's either that or camp in the open.

"Let's do it," you say. "Single file, Gagnon take the lead."

For twenty minutes Gagnon leads your troop in a weaving course through the jumbled field of crevasses and ridges. At times the sledges are perfectly safe with lots of room for maneuvering, at others you're right on the edge looking straight down hundreds of feet.

It's one of these scary times, when you're squeezing between two deep fissures, with little room to spare, that you see a glint of something down in the crevasse. You give the signal to stop and carefully work your way nearer the edge.

It looks like something made of metal, but you need to get closer to see it properly.

Taking an anchor bolt, you fire into the rock and clip

yourself on. Very slowly, you lean out over the edge and peer down into the yawning crack.

A first you can't quite tell what you're seeing. Then as your eyes adjust to the light, you realize you're seeing the back half of a spaceship. The front must be embedded in the rock, or missing altogether. The ships skin is covered in metallic scales that remind you of pango feathers. A series of portholes run down the ship's side. Near the rear, just in front of a large thruster, is an open portal.

You've seen drawings of ships like this in the story books your family use to read you when you were a child. But you always thought that the tales of the first Petronians arriving in spaceships were just myths.

This could be a great historical discovery.

"Grab me that cable launcher," you say to the nearest cadet. "We need to investigate this."

It doesn't take long before you've rigged up a sling so you can safely make your way across the cable to the ship.

The ship is much larger that it looks from the small portion sticking out of the rock. Rows of cryogenic sleep chambers line the walls and stretch off into the gloom.

You hear a scraping on the metal floor behind you. It's a wide-eyed Gagnon looking around.

"Wow this thing is amazing," he says.

You nod in agreement. "We'll make camp here tonight. Let's get the troop to tether the sledges and come across to the ship."

Gagnon looks around at all the empty sleep chambers.

"Good idea. There's certainly no shortage of beds."

Once everyone is safely across, some of the cadets set up a burner and heat broth. Others wander around the ship gawking at all the controls and pipes and wires and other equipment.

"Geebus," Piver says. "So, all the stories are true. Petronians did come from another planet."

You look at the funny little miner and smile. "It certainly looks that way."

Piver scratches his head and wander over to a row of symbols on the wall. He stares a moment and then turns to you. "I wonder what this says and why they came all this way?

You walk over and trace the unfamiliar symbols with your finger — *Victoria* LIFERAFT ELEVEN - PLANET EARTH 2108.

"Yeah I wonder."

Congratulations, you have reached the end of this part of the story. You have made an historical discovery that could change the history of your people.

It is time to make another decision. Do you:

Go back to the very beginning and try another path? **P1**

Or

Go to the list of choices and start reading from another part of the story? **P216**

You have decided to go to mining school.

Members of your family have joined the Highland Slider
Corps for generations, but you have always wanted to
become a miner and go prospecting. It's not that you don't
respect your family's traditions. It's just that the idea of
hunting for blue diamonds fills you with excitement. Ever
since your first science class at school, geology has
fascinated you. You even dream of finding blue diamonds.
Besides, miners get to play with all the best equipment.

Maybe you'll go prospecting around an active volcanic
vent and look for tyranium needle crystals. Although risky,
the rewards can be great. After all, where would the
Highlanders be without crystals to provide grip on the
slopes?

Maybe you'll dig for diamonds. How would a slider's
guide stick work without a diamond hook for stopping?
How would the communities bore tunnels in the nearly
impregnable black rock to create hydroponic growing
chambers and secure sleeping and defense pods?

You've always felt mining technology has been
responsible for keeping the Highlands free. Sure, the Slider
Corps protect the communities and keep them safe from
attack by the Lowlanders, but without the blue diamonds
and needle crystals, the Highland communities could never
have been built in the first place. Were it not for miners, the
only inhabitants of the Black Slopes would be colonies of
red-beaked pangos, cave-dwelling moon moths, and feral

packs of egg-eating morph rats.

For the first year at mining school, you've studied mineralogy, mine construction and planning, mechanical engineering, and safety procedures. You've learned how to operate the diamond bores needed to grind through the layers of dense black glass to get at the diamonds hidden in the rock below. You've learned about cable launchers, exploration methods, volcanism and geology as well as mathematics and mining history. Every possible technique has been drilled into you.

Soon you'll be going on your first field trip to test your newfound knowledge. On this trip you'll receive practical instruction on how to distinguish between areas that contain diamonds from those that don't, as well as learn how to get at them.

You've been packing you sledge all morning next to a boy named Piver who keeps cracking jokes. He is the only other person at mining school that comes from a slider family and because of that, the two of you have become friends.

Your sledges will carry a boring machine, lubricant, drills, blasters, rock screws, diamond picks as well as food, personal gear and other equipment.

"Where do you find a morph rat with no legs?" Piver asks you as he throws a cover over his load.

"I don't know. Where?"

"Exactly where you left it."

You shoot a look in Piver's direction and shake your head and groan. "That was so bad."

Piver chuckles anyway.

As the two of you finish securing your loads, you hear Piver giggling at something under his breath. He's a strange one, but you'd far rather be around someone who's laughing than a grump any day. And you must admit his silliness makes the time pass.

Each sledge weighs over two hundred pounds by the time it is fully packed and takes a crew of two or three sliders to maneuver it safely around the Black Slopes.

Linked transport, using slider guides, is really the only way to get around safely. Mining expeditions have tried going solo, but accidents are common and many end up crashing to the bottom. It is far safer with an escort.

Your group is heading off to the volcanic rim of Glass Mountain, an area rich in tyranium needle crystals, not far from the Pillars of Haramon.

"OK students, listen up," one of your instructors says. "You'll be leaving in an hour so make sure you've got everything on your checklist packed and tied down securely."

You look at the long list in your hand. There are so many things.

The instructor looks sternly at the group, making sure everyone is listening. "Now I have an announcement to make. Every mining expedition needs a leader so we are going to appoint one of you to be in charge of your group."

There is a hum of voices as the students speculate on who it will be.

The instructor walks over and looks you in the eyes. "Are you up for it?"

This has come as a big surprise. "I think so, sir," you reply.

"Good. You've been our top student this term so trust your instincts and work with your slider escort. I'm sure you'll do fine. The rest of you, follow your leader's instruction."

Piver comes over and slaps you on the back. "Congrats."

But the instructor hasn't finished. "Make sure you keep your picks and anchor guns close at hand. Not only is rain a possibility, there have been sightings of Lowland scouts in the last few weeks. You'll need to be ready to help your escort if required."

The thought of coming across Lowlanders while prospecting takes some of the fun out of the expedition and being the leader increases your responsibility even more.

Fifteen minutes later, a group of thirty sliders arrive. You are introduced to the lead slider and the two of you discuss the trip. You do a quick tour of the sledges and make sure each of the miners has packed properly and then return to double check your own.

Three sliders come over to your sledge. Two of them attach their harnesses to the front and one attaches to the back. The slider at the back introduces herself as Shoola. She's a strong looking girl in her late teens. You can see the muscles in her legs and arms through her close fitting uniform.

"You can climb aboard now," Shoola tells you. "We're about to head up the first tow."

You climb on top of the sledge and hook your boots under a strap, another you clip around your waist like a belt. These will keep you from falling off as the sledge is dragged up the steep towpath.

The sliders lock their boots into a stable sliding platform with a short metal bar that slides out the sole of their left boot and attaches to a notch near the instep of their right. Shoola, at the back of your sledge, will act as the team's brake.

As the front sliders get ready to clamp onto the tow, they stand with knees slightly bent. One positioned on either side of the quickly moving cable.

You look up the towline. A faint purple mist shrouds your view to the top. The low sun creates a light show as its rays reflect off the shiny, black rock.

"On my mark," the head slider calls out. "Three, two, one, go!"

The two front sliders throw their cable-clamps over the towline and squeeze down on its handle. As the clamps grip, the slack goes out of the strap running between the clamp and the sliders' harnesses. There is a short jerk, and the sledge starts moving.

The acceleration up the slope is exhilarating. You feel your abdominal muscles tighten in an attempt to keep yourself sitting upright. When you look back down the hillside, past Shoola, you see the other sledges racing up the towpath behind you.

"Yippee!" you yell. "What a ride!"

Up and up you climb until you enter the mist. The view disappears and the temperature drops. You reach for your flask and take a few gulps of hot broth. You secure the flask and grab a couple hard-boiled pango eggs to munch on. Turning around, you show an egg to Shoola. She nods and rubs her stomach. Tossing an egg in her direction, she deftly catches it one handed while easily keeping her balance and takes a bite.

Finally, your group emerges from the mist and you see a large motorized wheel whirling the cable around its belly and sending it back down the mountain.

The two sliders at the front of your sledge prepare to release their tow clamps and dismount. Shoola gets her guide stick into position, ready to drag its diamond hook to slow you all down.

You come to a screeching stop on a flat platform cut into the side of the mountain. Before the next group arrives, your group uses their sticks to push the sledge along a short path towards the bottom of the next tow.

While you wait for the sliders to clamp on to the next cable, you look around at the scenery. Now that you are above the mist the air is clear. You can see a long way. To the west and east, a towering range of mountains extend as far as you can see. To the north a braided river delta protrudes into a turquoise sea. On the flatlands, crops create a patchwork of green, yellow, orange and red, and wisps of smoke from cooking fires drift on the light breeze. Behind you, to the south, the slope keeps rising up towards the jagged skyline.

You are brought back to the present when you hear a slider start the countdown as they get ready to head up the next tow. Moments later you're off in a blur, rocketing higher up the mountain.

After repeating this process three times on three different tows, the training center has disappeared far below.

From the top of the last tow, your group turns to the west and takes a narrow path along the ridge. This will lead you to a slightly wider traverse path across an exposed face into the head of the next valley.

Once in this new valley, it should be a simple slide down to the next series of tows some seventeen miles away.

As you slide along, you dream of diamonds, sparkling, blue and translucent. You wonder if you'll be a success or if you'll go broke and end up back in your home community growing hydro. After all, if diamonds were that easy to find, everyone would be out looking.

By the time you reach the next tow, your backside is sore from sitting on the sledge. You are looking forward to getting off, stretching your legs, and having some food.

Off to your left, on the far side of the valley, is a sheer cliff dotted with bore holes. Specks of light flicker and flit about in the various openings.

You point. "Look, moon moths!"

"Wow, there must be a lot of them for us to see them

from way over here." Shoola says.

You pull out your scope and take a closer look, but even through the high-power lens you can't make out much detail being so far away. It's at night that the moon moths really shine. Their wings absorb sunlight and then at night their wings give off a shimmering blue glow.

Miners often capture moon moths and put them in little cages to use as a light source when their battery supplies run low. But you hate the idea of caging these beautiful creatures. It seems cruel somehow.

"Meal break," the lead slider says as the sledges pull up at the bottom of the next tow. "We leave in half an hour, so get some broth in you while you have a chance."

"And don't forget to tether your sledges," you say to the other miners, as you unbuckle yourself, climb down, and hook on to an anchor. "This ground may look flat but the slightest slope and anything not securely tethered will be off and away before you can stop it."

Once you're happy with your tether, you test out your needle boots. Unlike the sliders who are used to moving around the slopes, and have diamond spurs permanently fitted to their heels, your boots have far less grip so you need to be careful.

You eat some dried hydro and drink a cup of broth, and then start doing a few squats to stretch out your tight muscles.

Piver comes over and starts stretching next to you. As you exercise, you watch the humming cable disappear up the slope.

"This one looks even steeper than the last," you say.

Piver gives an excited jiggle. "I was talking to one of the sliders. He reckoned it's the longest tow in all of Petron. One thousand nine hundred vertical feet gained in less than fifteen minutes. Nearly a one in one gradient, no platforms, just straight up!" Piver's enthusiasm is contagious.

"Wow, that is steep," you say.

"See you at the top," Piver says. "It's all downhill from there."

You give him a thumbs-up and then start checking the straps on your sledge just in case something's come loose during the morning's run.

As you finish cinching the last belt, the lead slider clears his throat. "OK, everyone, mount up. We've still got some miles to cover before dark."

Just as you are about to climb onto your sledge a voice yells out.

"Take cover! Lowlanders!"

You and Piver duck down behind your sledges just as a small group of Lowlanders carrying a white flag come into view.

Off to your right the lead slider is forming his troop into an attacking formation.

Piver looks at you. "They're carrying a white flag. Why are the sliders getting ready to attack? As leader, aren't you going to say something?"

"Just give me a minute to think," you say.

84

It is time to make a quick decision. Do you:

Encourage the sliders to attack the Lowlanders? **P141**

Or

Yell out for the sliders not to attack so you can find out what the Lowlanders have to say? **P150**

You have decided to put extra safety precautions in place after the accident.

Hindsight is a wonderful thing, but anyone can look back. Sliders are supposed to plan ahead so accidents don't happen in the first place. You should have known that one cadet on the back of a heavy sledge wouldn't be enough to control its speed.

Dagma stays silent, but by the scowl on her face you can tell she has a poor opinion of your leadership. Not that you can blame her.

"New formation," you say. "Two cadets at the back of each sledge. We need more braking power."

Why didn't you do this from the beginning? If you had, you wouldn't have lost a full sledge of valuable supplies.

"I take full responsibility," you say. "But we can't let this get in the way of completing our mission."

Dagma can't help herself. "So we're going to go slow now are we? How is getting caught in the rain going to help our safety record?"

"Better to arrive a bit late than not at all," you say. "Besides, there's no sign of rain at the moment."

"At the moment..." Dagma mumbles while kicking her sledge with the toe of her boot.

Yes, choosing the fast route was a mistake. But learning from your mistakes is how one gains experience. You're not too proud to admit you were wrong and change your methods.

"Everyone is going to have to keep an eye out for Lowlanders now that we're all harnessed up," you tell the cadets. "It's a setback, but we have to keep positive."

Dagma starts to comment. "Knowing our luck we'll…"

"Enough, Dagma!" you snap.

Dagma looks at the ground and grinds her teeth, but she stays quiet.

You look back to the other cadets. "Get ready to move out. We need to keep going if we're going to make the Pillars of Haramon by dewfall."

Even the bright and usually cheerful Gagnon looks a little shaken.

"Gagnon, you'd better stay out in front. We can't afford to have our navigator in harness."

Gagnon nods.

"In fact, why don't you extend out a bit. Signal with your guide stick if you hit a tricky section, then the rest of us will be ready for it."

You tell the miner whose sledge was lost to climb aboard yours then give the signal to slide. "Remember, eyes front and hooks ready."

Gagnon takes off down the track. The rest of the group follows. The other miners sit nervously, eyes wide, watching the track, but helpless to do anything.

You know that before long you will come to the most technical part of the journey, a series of steep switchbacks, known as Zigzag Drop.

The new combinations are working well. At least now, if

one of the lead sliders slip, there are two others to stop the sledge and allow their fallen comrade time to regain their feet.

As you crest the broad ridge that leads onto the steep face of Mt Transor, and the start of Zigzag Drop, you call a brief halt.

The slope in front of you is dark and foreboding. Its black surface gives it the appearance of being smooth ... if only that were the case.

A well worn track, cut into the rock, and used by Highlanders over the centuries, runs like a ribbon back and forth down the hill. You can't believe how narrow it looks from the top.

On a plateau far below, a jumble of sharp ridges and crevasses, the results of a backwash of superheated black glass when the mountains were first formed, look dangerous enough to weaken the knees of even the most experienced Highland slider.

Going over the edge here would be fatal.

"Cadets, let's take this real easy," you say. "Scrape the mountainside with your loads if need be, the further you are from the edge the better. If a single runner goes over here, you'll be heading towards the bottom before you have time to correct. Believe me, if there was ever a time you don't want to be free sliding, this is it."

You are about to wave your arm for everyone to move out when you remember the wise words of one of your instructors. He spoke of leading by example. Now might be a time to do just that.

After unclipping your harness, you move forward, past the other sledges, until you reach the first in line. You put your hand on the front cadet's shoulder. "I'll take the lead sledge down. You go and take my spot at the rear."

The cadet breathes a sigh of relief and wastes no time unclipping his harness.

You connect to the steering runners on the front sledge and wave your arm. "Okay, let's move. Steady as we go. Cadets at the back, keep your hooks down. I don't want to be moving at anything more than walking pace until we get to the bottom."

You can feel the sledge wanting to take off, but whenever the speed builds, you turn the runners inward and let the overhanging bundle of mining equipment scrape the slope. This, and the heavy braking from the cadets at the rear, seems to be keeping the load under control … so far anyway.

The screech of diamond hooks on rock sounds like a flock of angry pangos fighting for scraps.

Before long you've traversed across the width of the face. The first switchback is coming up. You lift the toe of your front boot and dig a heel spur into the rock. The front of the sledge presses against your backside. You can hear hooks digging deep behind you as the sledge slows even more.

Just before you reach the apex of the turn, you stab the needle end of your guide stick into the slope and kick both heels, pushing firmly to your left. The nose of the sledge responds, its runners grip, and the cumbersome load slowly swings around the hairpin. Once safely past the corner you realize you've been holding your breath and suck gulps of fresh cool air.

"One down and thirteen to go," you mumble to no one in particular.

The second turn has been cut deeper into the rock leaving a knee-high barrier between you and the edge, but as soon as you are around the corner, the edge and the void beyond reappear. One hundred feet down the steep face, you see the track coming back the other way.

Sweat trickles down your forehead. A quick glance over your shoulder reveals the clenched jaws and wide eyes of the cadets behind you. You try to control your breathing. In through your nose and out through your mouth, slow and easy.

You were hoping the switchbacks would get easier as you went along, but that isn't the case. If anything they get harder. Your nerves jangle even more as you approach each new switchback. Your knees tremble. Some of the tremors are a result of the physical strain of sliding downhill, of holding back the weight of the sledge, but mostly your knees tremble in fear.

An instructor once told you that bravery isn't about not being afraid, it's about doing something despite your fear. Now that you're half way down the face … brave or not you've got no option but to continue.

When you finally round the last switchback you breathe a

sigh of relief and raise your arm, signaling everyone to stop. "Once we get around these crevasses we'll have a proper break."

After a brief rest, Gagnon leads off once more. Ten minutes later you come to a halt on a flattish area beyond the crevasse field.

You give the order for the miners to tether their sledges. "Well done everyone. Let's break out the hydro and light the burners. I don't know about you, but I could do with a cup of hot broth."

Gagnon and Dagma fill their cups and come to sit beside you as you drink.

"I'm pleased that's over," you say. "That was tough."

Gagnon smiles. Color has returned to his face. "Now it's just the run down Long Gully and we'll be at the Pillars."

"We should go back to one brakeman per sledge," Dagma says. "If we're going to run across Lowlanders, Long Gully is where it's most likely to happen. Having all the cadets in harness will make us too slow to react. We should send a scouting party ahead of the main group as a precaution."

Gagnon shakes his head. "The sledges are too heavy. Why don't we double-sledge? With two sledges linked together we could get by with three cadets at the back. That way we can move fast but still have 50 percent extra braking power when we need it."

Dagma's head is nodding in agreement. "And we'll still have some spare cadets to scout ahead for trouble," she says.

You like Gagnon's idea. "Sounds like a good compromise. You're the strongest Dagma, would you like to choose another three cadets and lead the advanced team?"

Dagma seems surprised at your display of confidence. "What should we do if we come across Lowlanders?"

"Assess their numbers. If there's only a couple, try to capture them. That way Command can question them once we reach the Pillars of Haramon. If there are more than two, wait for the rest of us to arrive. No point in taking unnecessary chances."

Dagma calls out the names of the cadets she wants for her advanced team.

"Don't get too far in front, Dagma. Remember our goal is getting everyone to the Pillars in one piece. Let's not make any more mistakes, okay?"

Dagma gives you a funny look. "Have I made any mistakes today?"

She's right … you're the one who's made mistakes. A good leader has to trust their team members. You'll never gain her respect if you don't trust her.

"No, and that's why you're in charge of the scouting party. You're one of the best scouts we've got."

Dagma stands a little taller with the compliment. The hint of a smile crosses her face for the first time today.

"Okay everyone, listen up. Dagma and her team are going to scout out front. Let's get these sledges reorganized. We've got to get to the Pillars before dewfall, and that means we need to get moving. Gagnon you act as guide for the rear group."

"Let's go," Dagma says, turning to her scouts.

Within a few minutes, Dagma's group are little more than charcoal dots on a black landscape.

The rest of the cadets are quick to reconfigure the sledges into pairs, a short cable linking them, one behind the other. One cadet clips on to the front of the front sledge and three cadets clip on to the back of the second sledge.

Long Gully is a slightly twisted half-pipe a quarter of a mile wide and sixty miles long. The idea is for the sledges to swoop back and forth down the valley in big sweeping S-turns using the natural contours of the gully to change direction and keep the sledges from gaining too much speed.

This part of the trip, assuming no Lowlanders are spotted, should be high-speed fun with little risk.

But things in the Highlands, are rarely simple, and never without an element of danger. To the south clouds are forming, pushing their way up the mountains from the interior. As the warm air rises, much of the moisture it contains fall as rain on the southern side of the divide but, unknown to you, some of the rain has crept over to the north and has begun to fall on the slopes high above you.

The first hint of danger is a trickle of water streaking the black rock on the far side of Long Gully. The water reflects silver in the afternoon light and is only a few yards wide, but there is no way you could run sledges through it without losing control.

Luckily one side of Long Gully is slightly lower than the

other. By sticking to the high side your group can continue to travel. But, depending on how much rain falls on the upper slopes, you know this harmless looking trickle could spread and become a deadly torrent in a short space of time. Once that happens, wherever you are, you'll have no option but to find a place to anchor yourself and ride it out until it's safe to move off again.

You wonder if Dagma and her scouts have seen the danger. If so, they should have stopped by now, but there is no sign of them. Where could they be?

You signal the troop to a halt. "We need to find a safe place to anchor," you say raising your arm and pointing towards the rapidly widening stream. "That water is spreading."

The other cadets are chattering nervously between themselves.

Gagnon slides over to your position. "According to the map, there are some abandoned mine shafts about a mile down the valley. If we keep left we should be able to make it to them before the water spreads to this side."

There is no time to wait. You must make up your mind quickly.

"Everyone follow Gagnon. We need to get to shelter right now," you order.

Gagnon pushes off and does a series of shallow turns, keeping to the left-hand side of the valley. The rest of you follow. The water is spreading as new rivulets form. The water isn't that deep, but it doesn't have to be deep to be dangerous on the Black Slopes of Petron.

"There they are!" a cadet yells out. "I see the portals!"

Gagnon has seen them too. With a stab of his stick, he pushes towards a pair of narrow entrances cut into the slope of the half-pipe.

Some old scaffolding, once used by miners prospecting for tyranium needle crystals, is bolted onto the rock nearby, but there is no sign of current habitation.

"Hurry!" you shout to Gagnon. The water is nearly here."

Gagnon points his front foot at the portal and pushes harder with his stick. You look behind and see that new streams are forming across the slope. It is going to be a close call.

When Gagnon disappears into the hillside, you breathe a sigh of relief. The rest of you are right behind him. As long as there are no surprises in the tunnel, your troop will be fine.

"Tether your sledges everyone, we could be in for a long wait."

Once you've secured your sledge, you have time to look around. When you look up, it's like looking at the night sky. Moon moths have taken over. After admiring their beauty, you turn to look back outside.

The clouds have rolled in from higher up the mountain. Now, misty rain is falling and the far side of the gully has disappeared altogether. Water rushes downhill, following the contours of the ground. Small rivulets join together to form torrents.

Where is Dagma? Are she and her group of cadets still out in this weather?

They must have anchored themselves to the hill somewhere further down. If they haven't found shelter somewhere, they will be in for an unpleasant night out in the open.

Then you hear a hollow sounding voice echoing from further along the tunnel.

"What kept you?" It's Dagma and her scouts. "Didn't you see the water coming?"

Typical of Dagma to boast.

"You did have a head start remember. I thought I told you not to get too far in front."

"We've been investigating," Dagma says, changing the subject. "There's a side tunnel that runs downhill. It could lead towards the Pillars. Maybe we should go that way?"

Gagnon pulls out his map. "It's an old tunnel that comes out a mile above the Pillars, but it's miles long and over a hundred years old. Who knows what condition it's in."

"I think we should try it out," Dagma says. "Otherwise we're stuck here doing nothing until the slopes dry. Boring!"

You're not a big fan of sitting around either. It would be great to get closer to the Pillars. Then your troop won't have so far to go once the rain lets up. Command did say the equipment was urgent.

But old tunnels can deteriorate over time, and they get colonized by morph rats. How do you know if it is safe? You also know that earthquakes still rumble from time to time as the molten core tries to force its way to the surface.

It is time to make a decision. Do you:

Try to get closer to the Pillars of Haramon by going down the tunnel? **P97**

Or

Stay put and wait for the slopes to dry before proceeding to the Pillars? **P99**

You have decided to go down the tunnel.

Moon moths light your way down the tunnel for the first mile or so, but as you and your troop get further into the tunnel, the moon moths become less frequent.

Before long you are forced to strap on headlamps so you can see where you're going. Slender veins of tyranium crystals streak through the black rock and make patterns along the walls as you slide.

Gagnon is back in the lead, with Dagma and her scouts close behind. The rest of your troop is sliding in formation behind them. In parts of the tunnel the slope is steep, requiring the dragging of hooks. Screeches fill your ears as they echo down the tunnel.

At first, you don't notice the trickle of water as it creeps down the tunnel behind you.

With every drop the rock you are sliding on becomes slicker. You need to put in an anchor bolt, and quickly. But to do that, you need to be stopped. All you can do at the moment is lean down on your hook and hope the ground levels out.

The rear sledges, caught by the water, are sliding faster than those in front. You hear a yell behind you. With moisture underfoot, nobody can slow down. You hear the sound of sledges colliding. Another cadet yells as she is knocked from her feet.

Will Gagnon and Dagma realize what is going on in time and be able to put in an anchor to stop the rest of you from sliding uncontrolled to the bottom of the tunnel in a jumble of bodies and equipment?

"Emergency anchors!" you yell at the top of your voice.

But it is too late. Water is rushing down the tunnel.

The sledge behind you smacks into your back and knocks you off your feet. You've made a huge mistake. Now your entire troop is heading towards the bottom of the tunnel in an uncontrolled slide.

Unfortunately, this part of your story is over. It was a poor decision to take your group down the old tunnel without checking it first. If you had, you would have discovered the tunnel had been damaged by earthquakes and that water would leak into it from the surface.

With luck some of your cadet might survive the pile-up at the bottom, but for you this part of your story has come to an end. Would you choose differently next time?

It is now time for you to make another decision. Do you:

Go back to the very beginning of the story and try another path? **P1**

Or

Go back to your last decision and choose differently? **P99**

You have decided to wait for the slopes to dry rather than go down the tunnel.

"We may as well light a burner and have some broth," you say to the cadets. "Who knows how long it will be before we can head out."

The others waste no time in getting a makeshift kitchen organized. A thin boy with blond hair comes to where you are sitting and hands you a steaming cup.

"Thanks," you say, leaning back against your pack and looking up as you sip. Hundreds of glowing moon moths hang from the ceiling

After finishing your broth you close your eyes and try to sleep.

The rain continues for the rest of the afternoon and most of the night. When you wake up and look outside it is just getting light. As the temperature rises, and the sun sneaks over the ridge, vapor rises from the black rock.

Thankfully, the sky is clear with no further sign of cloud.

"Okay everyone, the slopes are drying fast. We should be able to move out in less than an hour. Get some food into you and then get these sledges turned around and ready to go."

Everyone is keen to get moving again, especially Dagma, who helps light the burner and gives the other cadets a hand passing out broth and dried hydro.

"There might be a few damp patches on the slope, so let's hook up with two brakes per sledge," you say. "We don't want any accidents so close to the Pillars."

"But what about scouts?" Dagma says, disappointed to be back in harness.

You shake your head. "I doubt any Lowlanders will be left on the slope after that downpour. Better we play it safe."

Dagma shrugs and finds a spot at the back on one of the sledges.

When you feel the slopes have dried enough, you turn to Gagnon. "Shall we get out of here?"

The morning air is cool and clear, but already you can feel the warmth of the rock beneath you. Whatever dust was in the air has been washed away by the rain. You can see so far it's amazing.

The braided river delta far below sparkles like a diamond necklace. The ocean and horizon beyond seem closer somehow. Twenty miles further down Long Gully, you can just see the tops of the Pillars of Haramon poking above the surrounding terrain.

Gagnon pushes off and leads the group on a swooping path that takes you up one side of the valley and then across to the other.

You smile as you slide, the wind in your face, whipping at your hair. This is what you like best about being a Highland slider. It's the feeling you get as you race down a mountainside, the whole world spread out before you. It's being part of a group that will do anything to keep you safe and knowing you will do the same in return. It's the way a slider can use gravity to move with grace and speed with so little effort. It's the closest thing to soaring you've ever felt.

Before you know it, your troop is screeching to a stop outside the main portal of the northernmost pillar.

An officer is there to greet you. "Well done, cadets," he says. "Welcome to the Pillars of Haramon."

Congratulations, you have made it to the Pillars of Haramon. You've brought much needed supplies and equipment that will help keep your communities safe from the Lowlanders. This part of your mission is complete. But have you tried all the different paths the story can take? Have you gone mining? Fought off morph rats? Discovered the moon moths' secret?

It is time to make another decision. Do you:

Go back to the very beginning of the story and try another path? **P1**

Or

Go to the list of choices and start reading from another part of the story? **P216**

wind and rain have eroded them. Fissures and holes are dotted about their pitted surface.

In these cracks and crannies, hundreds of wild pangos have made their nests. You can see the bird's light grey bodies and shiny red beaks contrasting the dark rock as they crowd together, screeching and squabbling for the limited nesting spaces. At the base of one of the columns is a crude shelter used by egg hunters during the laying season.

During the breeding season female pangos sit on their eggs while the males fly many miles to the lowlands where they fill up with grain and fish before making the return journey to empty their gullets to feed the sitting females.

Once the clutch of pango eggs hatch, both parents make the journey each day, bringing back food for their babies until the young are able to fly and hunt for themselves.

Your attention is distracted from the pango colony by Gagnon waving and pointing down the slope to the right. It's Tow-Base 9. You can see the sun glinting off the tow's cable as it runs up the hillside.

You lower your guide stick and turn the sledge you are leading a little more to the right. A hand signal tells the cadets on the back to get ready to drag their hooks. Within minutes, your group is pulling up at the tow-base.

Some crew members have spotted you coming down the valley and have opened a portal. Pushing right once more, you allow the last of your momentum to carry the sledge neatly through the opening and into the parking bay bored deep into the rock.

Two members of the tow-base's crew are there to greet you.

Once your cadets are inside, a door glides shut with barely a sound. Thin slits in the outer wall provide just enough light for you to see a three-way junction about ten paces further on.

In typical Slider Corps fashion, single letters indicate where each tunnel goes. A indicates accommodation, H for hydro chambers, and D for the base's defensive positions. The Slider Corps have always been ones for simplicity.

"Okay everyone get your harnesses off and await instructions." You turn to the tow's crew and salute. "Troop 6-E reporting as instructed."

"Nice to see you made it, cadets," the older of the two crew members says. "We've had reports of Lowlanders in the valley."

As you tell them about your trip, one walks to a series of small holes bored in the smooth black wall. She shouts into one of them and then listens closely for the reply. You've heard about these communication pipes, but this is the first time you've seen them.

"Your troop is in accommodation pod 2," the crew member says. "I'll call ahead and let them know you're coming."

You are impressed with the base's method of communication. These holes must lead all over the base.

"Let's get you lot settled. Your gear can stay where it is."

You and your team follow the tunnel marked "A" deeper

into the hillside. Holes bored in the roof provide just enough light to see where you are going. Although long and dingy, the corridor eventually leads to pod 2. The pod is circular and has sleeping notches cut into the wall like those at the slider training base. But unlike the training base, the notches here are stacked three-high and there is not much extra space to store personal stuff. Not that you expected luxuries at an advanced base like this one.

The crew member waiting to assist your group to settle in is surprising in more ways than one. Firstly, she is taller than any of your group and secondly her flame-red hair makes you look twice. It has to be the brightest hair you've ever seen.

When Gagnon sees her, he can't help staring.

"Is there anything else I can get you?" the redhead asks.

You shake your head. "I think we can find our way around. This pod is laid out similar to our last one."

"I hear the Lowlanders are gathering," she says. "Sometimes they dip their arrows in pango poo you know. Boy, does that cause infection."

"Thankfully we carry antibiotics for that," you say.

"Just as well. Now, if you'll excuse me, I'd better get back to work."

Just as she is leaving, another crew member comes in with a trolley loaded with hydro and broth. The cadets and mining students are starving and descend on the cart like a pack of scavengers.

Just as you're finishing the last of your broth, a slightly

distorted voice echoes through a communication hole in the wall.

"Cadet Leader 6-E, please report to Defense One."

You're not exactly sure where Defense One is, but you know it will be down the "D" corridor somewhere.

When the message is repeated, you figure it must be urgent and waste no time in leaving the sleeping pod. When you reach the junction you turn into the D corridor. Not far along, the tunnel splits into four. Each is marked with a number. You take the first and start up a narrow set of steps cut into the pure black rock.

The staircase spirals around in a tight circle. You start counting each step as you go without even realizing it.

Defense One has a curved window of black glass, ground so thin it is almost clear. "Nice view," you say to a pair of officers sitting around a small table in the middle of the pod.

The window overlooks the entire valley. Wisps of smoke rise from the foothills far below where the Lowlanders have made their camp.

"It will be until I see those 20,000 Lowlanders marching up the valley," an officer says.

You gulp when you hear the number.

The officer does not look happy. "We've heard they've got some new machine that moves up the slope by drilling holes that allow a rotating sprocket on the front to grip the slope. Our scouts have seen them from a distance but that's about all we know. The machine our scouts saw was towing a hundred Lowlanders at a time. The Lowlanders must have found a new source of diamonds somewhere."

You start to say something, but then stop. This is a time to listen to those with more experience.

The officer has worry lines across his forehead. "We'll need more information if we're to send these machines to the bottom."

"So what is Troop 6-E to do, sir?"

"Tomorrow morning you will continue on to the Pillars of Haramon, as planned. If you see one of these machines along the way, your orders are to stop, watch, and in the event you spot a weakness, attack. We can't let the Lowlanders get above us. All our defensive positions are based on them coming at us from below. If one of these machines transports enough of their men up onto one of our main trails we could be in real trouble. Think your troop is up for that?"

You swallow hard. "Of course sir!"

"Okay. Best you get back to your cadets and get a good night's sleep. Tomorrow could be a long day."

That night you dream of shiny black pillars, and all the possible ways tomorrow might go. When the wake-up buzzer goes off, you bounce to your feet, keen to get going.

After a quick meal and toilet stop, you lead your troop back to the sledges and sort out the teams. This tow is steeper and longer than the others you've been on and there are no stops on the way up. It's just one long run to the ridgeline.

You check your harness and get ready to clamp on. The

cable is a blur as it whirls up the slope. "On my mark…"

As your clamp grips, you and your sledge start moving up the slope. You've been warned by the base's crew that the offloading platform at the top is narrow. Hopefully everyone will be alert. The last thing you want is for a team to overshoot the ridge and go plummeting down the other side.

The intensive cadet training has paid off and everyone arrives at the top in one piece. An officer is waiting.

"Now keep your eyes open," he says. "Remember, we know almost nothing about this new machine, so obtaining information is vital. Don't risk yourselves unless you see a weakness you can exploit. Good luck."

You salute and order your troop move off along the ridge. This narrow track will lead you to a traverse that runs towards the top of Long Gully. Then it's down Long Gully to the Pillars of Haramon, some fifty-two miles from where you are standing.

Once again Gagnon takes the lead. Everyone handles the traverse track well, but when you turn into Long Gully proper, you spot something you've not seen before.

A series of angled holes have been bored into the rock. As you inspect the holes you can just imagine how a machine, fitted with a large rotating sprocket, could move up and down these holes without any problem. Each tooth on a sprocket would have a corresponding hole for it to lock in to. The machine could climb as fast as the wheel could rotate and a drill could drill.

You fit your guide stick into one of the holes and the toe

YOU SAY WHICH WAY

of your boot in another and take a step up. At least you and your cadets can use this track to gain altitude as well.

But that doesn't change the disturbing fact that one of these Lowland machines is above you. This is exactly what the officer at the tow base was afraid of. Should you follow the track and try to gain vital information? Or is the equipment you're transporting more important? You can see merit in both courses of action.

It is time to make one of the most important decisions of your command. Do you:

Go up the mountain and scout out the Lowlanders' new machine? **P123**

Or

Take the vital equipment to the Pillars of Haramon? **P137**

You have decided to send some advanced scouts to test the route first.

Sending advanced scouts to check the route makes sense. Advanced scouts will enable you to see any Lowlanders that may have infiltrated the area before they see you, and more importantly, while you are still above them. Altitude is a critical advantage when on the Black Slopes of Petron.

Rather than sending Dagma out, you choose to lead a small group yourself. Now that you know Lowlanders are daring to come up the mountains, you want to be in a position to make quick decisions.

"Gagnon, come with me. Dagma, you hang back with the others and wait for my signal."

Dagma frowns. You can tell she hates being left at the rear. "So we all need babysitting now do we?" she mumbles.

It annoys you that Dagma isn't a team player. Why does she have to make snide comments under her breath? What good will that do the troop?

"Shut it, Dagma," you say. "One more word and I'll put you on report."

"You wouldn't…"

"… just try me!"

Dagma, so often the dominant personality in the troop, isn't used to being told what to do. Her mouth begins to open, but no words come out. Instead, she looks down at her feet in silence.

The other cadets snicker.

"Right, Gagnon, let's get going. The rest of you wait for my signal before sliding down to our position."

You relock your boots, put your front foot forward and push off with you guide stick. Gagnon follows. The soft hiss of boots on rock is all you can hear.

You aim towards the far right-hand side of the gully where you'll get a clear view down the slope. Once there you sweep left in a gentle arc towards the center again.

It's amazing how quickly you progress down the slope. Within a few minutes the cadets look like toys in the distance.

You drag your hook and come to a stop. Then you pull out your scope and look down the slope.

"All clear," you say to Gagnon.

You know Dagma will be impatiently studying you through her scope. You wave an arm and signal her and the other cadets to slide down and join you.

At first, the vibration under you feet is barely noticeable. You attribute your slight loss of balance to a gust of wind. But when the second tremor shakes you off your feet, you realize it's an earthquake.

You pull the anchor gun from your belt and fire a bolt into the rock. Both you and Gagnon clip on as quickly as possible. There may be more to come.

As suspected, the first jolts were pre-shocks to the main event.

A low rumbling is approaching, getting louder and louder as it does so. When the wave of energy reaches the surface a huge crack appears in the slope above you, ripping the gulley in half from one side to the other and creating a gaping crevasse between you and the cadets sliding down the slope towards you.

The shaking goes on for over a minute. The crack widens. How deep it goes is hard to tell from your position, but you have no doubt it will be deep enough to severely injure, if not kill, anyone falling into it.

You get your scope out of its pouch and focus on the cadets above. Some have fallen. There is nothing you can do apart from shout a warning and hope they manage to stop in time.

Another aftershock hits you, nearly as big at the first jolt. The dots above are getting bigger. You hear screeching. When the shaking stops and you manage to focus your scope again, you see that many cadets are still off their feet desperately trying to get up.

Standard procedure in these situations is to turn your sledge side-on to the slope to stop its downward momentum, but to do that, the cadet steering the sledge needs to be in control. That is impossible when you are on your backside free sliding down the hill. Sledges are skewed. One sledge is on its side dragging its crew down the hill behind it.

Before long those above are close enough for you to pick out individual faces. Dagma is nearest. Her large frame stands out from the crowd. She is still on her feet with her hook hard down. Her sledge has nearly stopped. For once

Dagma rushing off in front is an advantage. Thankfully the others sliding behind her are still much further up the slope.

You hear the pop of an anchor gun as Dagma fires a bolt into the rock. In a flash her sledge is tethered and she is looking back over her shoulder figuring out how to stop the others.

A couple of the sledges are slowing due to good work by their crew, but two are out of control and gaining speed. They are now within a quarter of a mile of the yawning chasm angling across the slope below them.

Another rumble passes up from below. The edge of the huge crevasse cracks and sends sharks of black glass plummeting down into it.

Your eyes are riveted on the drama above. You hear another two pops in quick succession, as more cadets manage to anchor their sledges.

Dagma quickly shrugs off her harness and slides across the slope, pulling a cable behind her. She crosses the path of the two out of control sledges sliding down towards her. Once she's gone far enough she fires another anchor bolt into the ground and wraps the cable around it.

"She's trying to snag the runners of those two runaway sledges," you say to Gagnon.

"Will it be strong enough?" Gagnon asks.

"We'll know in a couple of seconds." You cross your fingers and hope Dagma's plan works.

When the runners of the first sledge slide under the cable you can see the line begin to stretch. The sledge's momentum slows, but in the process the sledge skews sideways.

Dagma fires another anchor bolt into the slope and wraps the excess cable around it.

The cable seems to be holding, but the sledge is now side-on to the slope and starting to tip over.

"It's going to roll!" Gagnon yells.

Just as the sledge reaches tipping point, the second sledge hits the cable.

The extra stretch its impact provides drops the first sledge back onto its runners long enough for the cadets harnessed up to it to get their own anchors in. Thankfully the second sledge is going slower than the first. Its runner slides under the cable and it comes to an abrupt, but satisfying halt.

"Wow that was close," you say.

"You're telling me," Gagnon says. "But what now?"

You look up at the tangle of sledges and their shaken passengers. A huge crack lies between you and the rest of your troop. To your right the crack runs slightly downhill, across the slope and all the way to the cliffs beyond.

To your left the crevasse runs to the far side and up the opposite slope for nearly fifty yards terminating in a steep bluff. There is no detour around the crevasse that way. You have no option but to find a way across.

You and Gagnon start working your way back up the slope towards the newly formed crevasse. Dagma has clipped on to a line and is abseiling down to check out the obstacle from above.

The crevasse is deep. The gap between you and your troop is about five yards.

"What now?" Dagma yells out across the void.

That is a very good question. You could sling a cable and get your cadets across the gap, but the heavy and cumbersome sledges are a different proposition altogether.

You would fail in your mission if you left all this valuable equipment on the slope when it is so desperately needed at the Pillars of Haramon.

One of the miners has abseiled down to where Dagma is standing.

She secures herself and then looks at you across the empty space. "Can I make a suggestion?" the miner says.

"Sure," you say, happy to have some ideas come your way.

"If we put a series of anchor bolts on both sides of the crevasse, we can use mineshaft props to build a makeshift bridge."

"Would it hold the weight of a sledge?"

"No problem," the miner says.

You look at Gagnon. He nods.

"Okay," you say. "Let's do it."

It takes about an hour for the miners to get the metal bridge bolted together. It looks like a big ladder made from pipe. Then you've got the tricky job of maneuvering the bridge across the crevasse and anchoring it securely to both sides.

Once it's secure, the runners of a sledge should be able to

slide across the ladder without falling through the gaps ... in theory at least.

Each sledge has a steering lever that can be controlled from onboard so the crew can climb aboard and ride across. The sledges speed can be slowed by a cable attached to a belay point on the uphill side.

The first trip across the bridge is a nervous affair.

"Geebus that's a long way down!" Piver says once the sledge he's riding is safely across.

Once all the sledges have crossed, a miner comes over to you. "I'm pretty sure I saw a vein of diamonds in that crevasse as I was crossing."

"Really? You've got good eyes."

"Light reflects differently off diamonds. It's just a matter of knowing what to look out for."

You look at the miner and wonder if he knows what he is talking about. But then if anyone is to know about diamonds, it makes sense that it would be a miner. Why would he make this up? In fact, why would he tell you about the diamonds all? He could just come back at some time in the future and keep them all for himself.

"So why are you telling me?"

"You sliders saved my life. I was on that sledge heading for the crevasse."

Of course, one of the sledges Dagma saved.

The miner continues. "I think we should take some samples and stake a claim. We can all share it. Imagine how rich we'll be."

He has a point. Finding a vein of blue diamond would be big news and big profits. Few of the cadets come from wealthy families. Nobody joins the Slider Corps for the money.

"Can we do that?" you ask.

The miner shows you a sparkling row of teeth. "Yep. We sure can. I'll get my climbing gear and some survey pegs, okay?"

"Sounds like a plan," you say, eager to find out if what the miner says about the diamonds is true.

It only takes ten minutes to rig up a harness so the miner can safely abseil down into the crevasse. Attached to his belt are a hand pick, collection bag, impact drill, and pry rod.

"Dewfall isn't that far away," you tell the miner before he goes over the edge. "You've got fifteen minutes to get what you need. After that, we're pulling you up."

The miner nods, leans out over the void and walks backwards down the sheer wall of stone, letting out cable as he goes. When he gets to the layer he spotted earlier he stops and starts chipping away.

You lie on your belly and look over the edge. "Are they diamonds?"

"Sure are. Number 1s by the looks of them," he yells back.

Number 1s are top grade, used for making the hooks on guide sticks and drills for boring holes in the tough black glass.

After a few more minutes you yell down again. "Okay

time's up. We need to get going."

Half a dozen cadets start hauling on the cable. Before long, the miner and his collection bag are back on the surface.

"Have a look," the miner says.

You hold out your hand and he pours a number of sparkling blue stones into your palm.

"They don't look much in their raw state," he says. "But once they've been polished, you'll barely be able to look at them without some sort of eye protection.

You are lost for words. They are beautiful, alive with light, glowing softly in your hand.

"Wow," you finally get out.

It takes some discipline to take your eyes away from the mesmerizing sight, but you know you need to get your troop down to the tow-base ... and soon. Dewfall is fast approaching.

"Are you just going to leave the ladder here?" Dagma asks.

"Yes," you say. "If we need to get back across in a hurry, it will come in handy."

Dagma grunts and attaches her harness to the back of a sledge.

"Oh and well done Dagma, you did a great job saving those runaway sledges. I'm going to recommend you for an award when we get to the Pillars of Haramon. You deserve one."

The others overhear your comments and congratulate her

too. For the first time during the trip, you see her smile.

You give Dagma her moment in the sun, but when you look back up the slope you can see wispy clouds forming near the tops. "Okay, let's get moving. We've still got a few miles to go and it's starting to look like rain."

The aftershocks have stopped. After sliding for another hour or so without incident, Gagnon yells and points down the slope to the right. It's your destination.

As the last of the sun reflects off the oiled cable from Tow-Base 9, you lower your guide stick and turn your sledge a little more to the right. Then you signal the cadets at the back to begin dragging their hooks.

Someone has spotted you coming down the valley and has opened a portal. Pushing right once more, you allow your remaining momentum to ease the sledge neatly through the entry and into the parking bay bored into the rock. The others are right behind you.

Two members of the tow-base's crew are there to greet you. They guide the troop to its sleeping pod where a meal has been prepared.

The next morning your troops make their way up a long tow, along the ridge and then into the head of Long Gully. Sixty miles down this picturesque valley are the Pillars of Haramon and your final destination.

You imagine turning up with your troop, a bag of number 1s and a $1/40^{th}$ share in what could be one of the biggest finds of diamonds in recent times.

The miner who spotted the vein of diamonds in the

crevasse has transferred to your sledge, and he's been giving you a crash course in prospecting and mine management while you travel. It's amazing how finding diamonds has sparked an interest you never realized you had.

By mid afternoon the next day, your troop is pulling up outside one of the Pillars.

An officer greets you with a salute and directs you and your cadets to their accommodation pod. The miners get busy unpacking the much needed equipment for improving defensive positions and creating more magnifying disks to fight off invasion.

You climb up a narrow set of stairs to the top observation pod where you are debriefed by Command. While you are there you register the mining claim you've pegged out on behalf of your cadets and the student miners.

"Looks like everyone's hit the jackpot," the officer says. "Once tax is taken out, you should be left with a tidy profit."

You think about the officer's words and realize you *have* hit the jackpot. You're doing something you love. The profit you make from your share of the diamonds means you can help your family out, and you're standing a thousand feet above one of the most beautiful landscapes on the planet. What's not to like about that?

From high up in the observation pod you can see a patchwork of fields on the Lowlands below. Bright purples, greens, pinks and oranges create a mosaic of color across the flats towards the delta where braided rivers shimmer like necklaces as they meander back and forth. Beyond the delta, the ocean stretches off into the horizon.

You've heard stories about the ocean and wonder what it's like to swim in so much water. You wonder what it's like to be a Lowlander, to walk around on flat ground, where there isn't any danger of slipping and sliding to the bottom. Then you look back towards the towering Black Slopes of home and you realize you're happy where you are. Like generations before you, you are a Highlander, and proud of it.

Congratulations, you have reached the end of this part of your story. You have made it successfully to the Pillars of Haramon with your precious cargo and you have a share in a diamond mine. Well done!

But have you followed all the possible story lines? Have you gone mining, found tunnels, heard the cry of the wild pango, been attacked by morph rats? Discovered the secrets of the moon moth? It's time for another decision. Do you.

Go back to the very beginning of the story? **P1**

Or

Go to the list of choices and starting reading from another place? **P216**

**You have decided to go up and scout out the new
Lowland machine.**

The track is nothing more than a series of fist-sized holes
drilled into the slope. It runs straight up the mountain. Each
hole is a perfect fit for the toe of your boot so it should be
no problem following the track uphill.

The sledges are another matter. There is no way you can
take them with you. Nor do you want to leave them
unattended where another Lowland patrol might find them.

You'll have to split your troop up. But how many cadets
should you leave behind to guard the sledges? Maybe rather
than having them wait, you should send the sledges on down
to the Pillars of Haramon with the mining students while a
smaller group chases this machine.

You decide that three heads are better than one when it
comes to making decisions.

"Dagma, Gagnon, we need to talk."

The two cadets unclip from their sledges and slide over.

You look once more at the track running up the hill.
Then you take your glove off and stick your hand in one of
the holes. The rock is still slightly warm from the friction of
being drilled. The machine can't be too far away.

"What do you think? Should we split up and get the
miners down to the Pillars while the rest of us check this
out?"

Gagnon's gaze follows the track up the slope. He shakes
his head. "Weirdest thing I've ever seen. It must be quite a

contraption to be able to cut into the rock like this."

"Let's go up and get them," Dagma growls. "I'm not afraid of Lowlanders and their stupid machine!"

Once again Dagma is overflowing with raw emotion. Is it clouding her judgment? You wonder if she will ever realize that being afraid is okay. Real bravery is about doing what you must, despite your fear, not rushing at things like a demented morph rat.

You wish you had more time to consider things, but the time is passing. Your troop must get to the Pillars of Haramon before dewfall makes the slopes impossible to travel.

"I'm thinking most of our group should keep sliding down the valley towards the Pillars. A small scouting party will be less visible from above. If we can find out what the Lowlanders are up to, we might even come up with a plan to stop them."

Gagnon nods. "Sounds like a good idea. You have to walk softly to catch a pango."

"What?" Dagma snarls at Gagnon. "Why are you talking about pangos?"

Gagnon shakes his head and shrugs.

You turn to Dagma. "He means we need to move slowly and cautiously."

"Well why didn't he just say that?"

You ponder things a moment. "I agree with Gagnon. If we're going to get any useful information there's no point in rushing blindly up the hill just to get captured and end our days picking grain on some Lowland penal farm."

Your mind is whirling with options. Do you want Dagma on this expedition or should you send her down to the Pillars with the miners? What if she loses control and does something stupid?

"Okay. Listen up everyone," you say, "I'm sending the majority of you on to the Pillars of Haramon. Gagnon you'll be in charge."

Most of the miners seem relieved to be heading towards safety. You have little doubt the level headed Gagnon will get them there in one piece.

"Dagma, myself and two other cadets, will scout up the hill and try to find out what the Lowlanders are up to. If they spot us, we'll free slide back down as quickly as possible and catch up with you." At least with Dagma by your side, you can keep an eye on her. "Gagnon get going. We want this equipment as far from the Lowlanders as we can get it."

After picking two of your fittest cadets, you prepare to start the chase. "I hope you all feel like climbing," you say to your small group, "because it's all uphill from here."

Over your shoulder you hear Gagnon give the order for the sledges to move out.

You look at your three cadets. "We'll take turns leading. One will climb then the others can zip up to conserve their strength. That way we won't have to stop for breaks. It's the only way we'll have any chance of catching up with this machine of theirs. I'll go first. Get ready to move."

Without waiting for comments from the others you grab

a cable and climb rapidly up the line of holes provided by the Lowland machine. After a hundred quick steps, you stop and belay the others who clip their battery-powered zippers onto the light-weight cable. The tiny, but powerful rotor whirls and the cadets are quickly dragged up the hill.

"Dagma, you climb next," you say.

She takes hold of the cable and repeats the procedure, sprinting up the hill like it's a race. When Dagma reaches the end of the cable and has a secure belay in place, you and the other two cadets clip on and zip up to her.

By taking turns doing the hard uphill slog, it isn't long before the four of you have made considerable progress up the mountainside. When you reach the highest point on the ridge, the machine's tracks turn west.

You pull out your scope. In the distance you see the Lowland machine steaming along. A mechanism mounted on an extendable arm in front of the machine is drilling the track holes with quick precision. Behind the drill is a big sprocket with pointed teeth that fit neatly into the pre-drilled holes. As this sprocket rotates, it pulls the machine along the smooth rock on its long metal runners.

The machine has armored sides with viewing holes along its length and there is some sort of spring loaded mechanism on top and piles of cable. These must be the nets you've heard about.

Sitting on top of the machine are Lowlanders.

The machine is also towing a cable with at least thirty more Lowland troopers clipped on to it. How many

Lowlanders are inside the machine is anyone's guess.

You and the other cadets lie on the ground and study the scene before you.

"Where do you think they're going?" Dagma asks.

You pull a map from a pouch in your utility belt and spread it out on the ground before you. "They must be heading toward the Haramon Reservoir," you say. "All the settlements north and west of here, not to mention the base at the Pillars, rely on that water."

"Do you think they are going to poison it?" Dagma asks.

"I don't know. But we need to find out."

Protecting the Haramon Reservoir has never been a priority. Lowlanders have never been able to get this high up the mountain before, so security is minimal.

"What are we going to do?" Dagma asks.

"We're going to think of a way stop to them," you say. You turn to the cadets crouched behind you. "I need you two to slide back down and let those at the Pillars of Haramon know what is going on, just in case Dagma and I get captured or injured. Can you do that?"

"Yes," they say in unison.

"Well get going. It's important that they know that their water supply might be compromised, so be safe and get there in one piece."

You would have liked to have kept one of the two cadets with you, but you know that traveling in a pair is always safer than going solo. The two cadets waste no time in locking their boots together and sliding off down the slope.

You and Dagma resume your study of the Lowland machine through your scopes.

After a few minutes you put your scope down. "Any ideas, Dagma?"

"There are so many of them," she says. "We might be able to handle a few, but…"

For the first time Dagma's voice seems a little shaky. You lift your scope again, hoping you'll see something that Dagma has missed.

The machine is making steady progress along the ridge towards the next valley where the reservoir is located. As you follow the ridgeline with your scope, you notice there is one point where it narrows to little more than the width of the machine. A plan begins to form in your mind.

"How much do you reckon that machine weighs, Dagma?"

"I don't know. A ton and a half at least … plus the weight of the crew and those riding on top."

"So that's maybe four thousand pounds altogether. What do the thirty Lowlanders being towed behind it weigh?"

As you wait for Dagma's answer you do some calculations in your head. Thirty times an average weight of 150 pounds per Lowlander is 4500 pounds, a little more that the weight of the machine, its crew and passengers.

"If we can somehow push the troopers being towed over the edge just as the machine reaches that pinch-point on the ridge, do you think their combined weight will be enough to pull the machine over?"

Dagma considers what you've said a moment and then grins. "It's worth a crack. Once the first few are knocked off, it might start a chain reaction that takes them all."

"Stealth and timing will be everything. If they hear us coming, we'll be pin cushions before we even get close."

"You'd better follow me then," Dagma says with a grin. "I'll make a good shield."

As crazy as her comment sounds, it actually makes good sense. At least with Dagma in front, if you're spotted the mission still has a chance of success.

"You're crazy, Dagma. Brave, but crazy."

Once again you look through your scope and calculate the distance the machine has to travel to the narrowest part of the ridge. Then you estimate how far it is from your current position to the Lowlanders being towed.

At the current rate of progress the machine will be in position in about one and a half minutes. That gives you less than a minute to come up with a better plan or change your mind.

You look at Dagma. "We've got to decide now. Are you sure you want to do this?"

An evil grin crosses Dagma's face as she reverses her pack so that it protects her chest. "Does a morph rat stink? Let's send these pango-headed fools to the bottom."

You were afraid she'd say that. You've already started counting down in your head. After one last look through the scope you pack it away and get ready for the slide of your life.

"Tuck in behind, hands on my waist," Dagma says. "Let's go in low, fast and quiet."

"You have the lead, cadet," you say unhooking your boots and crouching down behind Dagma's bulk.

Dagma places her guide stick on the ground ready for a big push. "On my mark, three, two, one…"

Both of you push off as hard as you can and tuck into a low crouch. Only subtle adjustments are needed to keep you heading down the ridge towards the Lowlanders.

The wind is cool against the skin on your face as you peer over Dagma's shoulder. With every second, you gain speed.

When you are forty yards away, a Lowlander riding on top of the machine spots you and raises the alarm, but it is too late to save the last Lowlander from being slammed over the edge and down the steep slope. Before the next trooper has time to brace, he too is plucked off the ridge. The first two jerk the next one off his feet and over the edge, then another, and another.

You and Dagma drag your hooks to a stop and watch the perfect chain reaction unfold.

Now it's only a question of whether their combined weight will be enough to dislodge the machine.

You hold your breath as the last of the towed Lowlanders goes over. The weight on the rope has pulled the machine's rear end off line. Its rear runners are inching closer and closer to the edge.

Just as the machine starts to topple, the troops on top shift their weight to the opposite side from where the troopers have gone over. The machine teeters on the brink.

With a squeak, the back door of the machine flies open. You expect to see more troopers jumping out and attempt to stabilize the machine, but those fleeing the machine are too small to be troopers.

"The machine's full of children," you yell out to Dagma.

This is not at all what you expected. What are the Lowlanders doing with a bunch of children way up here?

"We've made a mistake Dagma. We've got to help."

Before you have time to stop her, Dagma has pushed off and is sliding towards the machine. She pulls a light-weight cable from her belt and forms it into a loop.

As she nears the back of the machine she throws the cable over a bracket and then turns and plummets over the opposite side of the ridge to where the Lowland troopers have fallen.

Seconds later you hear the familiar pop of an anchor gun.

The machine's runners edge closer to the sheer drop. Voices of struggling Lowlanders call out from below. You hold your breath as the cable Dagma has hooked onto the machine stretches tight.

You understand what she's done and why and slide down to help. You throw another cable around a handrail along the side of the machine and shoot a bolt into the rock.

Lowland children mill about wondering what to do. The machine has stabilized, but any false step could send one these youngsters down the steep face on either side of the ridge.

The right-hand side of the machine is almost at the edge, but at least the machine isn't moving now due to the anchors you and Dagma have put in on the other side.

Then you see Dagma's head appear above the ridgeline as she climbs back up the cable. When she reaches flat ground she flops down and heaves a huge sigh.

"Phew, that was exciting," she says, wiping the sweat off her forehead.

As you move towards Dagma, the adult Lowlanders work frantically to get their machine stabilized. A few Lowlanders look in your direction, but you are no longer a threat. Besides they are too busy securing the machine and keeping the children safe to worry about you.

"Should we take off?" Dagma whispers, her inherent distrust of Lowlanders coming to the surface once more.

"I want to find out why they have children up here. Something strange is going on. But if you want to make a run for it, feel free."

Dagma shrugs and stays where she is. "Best we stick together, don't you think?"

A few minutes later a Lowlander comes over to where the two of you are sitting. "I suppose you want to know what's going on," he says.

"We thought you were going to poison our water supply," you say as you stand to face him. "But then we saw the children and realized we'd jumped to conclusions."

"Understandable I suppose," the Lowlander says. "We've not had the best of relationships with you Highlanders over recent years."

"So why are you up here?" Dagma asks. "We nearly sent you all to the bottom."

"We're refugees from the delta. We escaped by stealing one of the Lowland army's new machines. We found some old uniforms to put on to keep warm. We're not used to the chilly mountain air."

You look around and notice that many of the Lowlanders are women. Normally Lowland troops are male. Then you see the patched elbows and frayed cuffs.

This ragtag bunch is made up of family units. It's not a troop of fighters at all.

"The Lowlanders are trying to force our men to fight. But we have no quarrel with the Highlanders. We are all the same blood after all. We just want a peaceful life, shelter, food and happiness for our children."

"Sounds fair enough, but where do you plan to go?" you ask.

"We are going to resettle on the far side of the mountains. We hear there are good pastures in the interior."

You nod. "Yes, I've heard that too. Still, that's quite a dangerous slide, especially with children and without trained people to escort you."

"What other choice do we have?"

You can understand his position. Lowlanders that refuse to fight are put into penal farms and used as forced labor. Nobody in their right mind would want that as a life.

"I have an idea," you say to the man.

The Lowlander seems interested. "I'm willing to listen if you can suggest something that will keep my family safe."

"We Highlanders are in much the same position as your family. We just want a peaceful life without interference from the Lowland Council. But unless we can come up with a way to defeat these new machines of theirs, we will have no option but to cave in to their demands."

"They are formidable machines," the Lowlander says. "They move uphill very fast and fling nets to entangle anyone who gets too close. Your Slider Corps will struggle to defeat them."

This is exactly what you were thinking.

"What if I guaranteed you safe passage and a slider escort down the mountain to the interior, in exchange for this machine? Both of us would gain. Yes?"

"Hmmm…"

You can see the Lowlander thinking.

His eyes close a little and his head bobs up and down. You hope he goes for the deal. For Slider Command, having one of these new machines to study would be a great advantage in the conflict that is sure to come.

A few seconds later he looks you in the eye. "You are very clever for one so young."

You smile at his compliment but remain silent.

"I like this plan of yours," he continues. "A strong Highland force will act as a buffer between our settlement and the Lowlanders. We would be able to trade too, our crops for your minerals and hydro."

"It sounds like we're in agreement then?" you say.

"Yes, I think we are," the man says.

"Okay, I think the first thing to do is to get your people settled. You can stay at the reservoir while I go back and organize some sledges and sliders to take you and your people down the mountain. There is a small base by the reservoir that has a spare accommodation pod. It might be crowded but at least you'll be safe."

The Lowlander nods his understanding.

"Some of your men can help us get this machine down to the Pillars of Haramon. Then within a few days, I'll send enough sliders and sledges back to get you all safely down the other side."

You hold out your hand to the Lowlander. "It will be nice to have some Lowland friends for a change."

"I agree," the Lowlander says. "We all bleed green, do we not?"

"Indeed we do," you say, "greener than the yolk of a pango's egg."

Congratulations, you have reached the end of this part of the story. You successfully obtained a Lowland machine for Slider Command to study, and made allies of a group of Lowlanders that will enrich your community.

Well done! But have you tried all the possible paths yet? Have you gone mining or found of the secret of the moon moths?

It is time to make another decision. Do you:

136

Go back to the very beginning of the story and try another path? **P1**

Or

Go to the list of choices and start reading from another part of the story? **P216**

You have decided to take the equipment to the Pillars rather than follow the Lowland machine.

You have decided to carry on to rather than go investigate the track the Lowland machine has made.

The officer told you that if you came across the machine you were to investigate, but this isn't the machine, it is just the machine's track. Why risk your troop? You can't take the sledges up the mountain, and for you to follow the track you'd have to split your troop into two sections which would only make each group weaker.

After unclipping your harness, you take out your scope and scan the upper slopes for any sign of the Lowlanders, but the track disappears over a ridge and there is no sign of the machine.

"Are we going after them?" Dagma asks. "We've got to do something."

"But how far up are they? They could be miles ahead. And if their machine climbs as quickly as we think, how do we know we'll even be able to catch them?"

Gagnon has heard your discussion and has pushed his way back to your position. "We can't let them get above us. Advantage comes with altitude, you know that. They could slide right down on us."

You bang your stick on the ground. "Our job is to get this mining equipment to the Pillars, not go chasing machines. I've made my decision."

Dagma looks at Gagnon and shakes her head. You hear

the hiss of air as she inhales through her teeth.

"You're making a mistake," Gagnon says. "Please reconsider."

You glance up the slope once more. Maybe by rotating climbers, and using zippers to drag you up the mountain you could catch the machine, but you hesitate. What if you waste precious time climbing up and the real danger is coming from below? How are you to know?

"Let's take a vote," Gagnon says.

"Yeah." Dagma looks at the other cadets in the hope that a stare will make them agree with her.

"This is not a democracy," you say. "I'm in charge and my decisions are final."

The cadets don't seem happy with your last statement — Highland communities value consensus above all else. Having their opinion ignored is a pet hate of all Highlanders.

"Yes, let's vote." You hear a few other cadets say.

"Seems the others want a say in this too," Dagma grunts.

"No. Get ready to move off."

Before you manage to clip on, Dagma sees her chance. With a sweep of her stick, she knocks you off your feet. Then she pushes you down the slopes with all her strength.

Before you know it you are free sliding down the hill, gaining speed as you go.

You try to regain your feet where you might have some control, but the ground is uneven and whenever you try to stand, a bump in the ground knocks you flat once more.

Spinning around you sit up with your feet out in front of

you. Leaning down on your hook you try to slow your speed, but before you can come to a complete stop you hit a steeper patch and take off again. Further ahead you see a series of knife-edged ridges. If you hit one of those it will cut you to ribbons.

You have two choices. Try to stop, or use your stick to steer and avoid the danger below.

You dig in your heel spurs and jab your stick, pushing yourself further into the centre of the gully away from the dangers on its left. You are moving too fast for your equipment to slow you down. None the less, you lean down hard on your hook. After the steep patch the ground levels out and you manage to stop, but by then the rest of your troop is well out of sight.

Being isolated on the slope is not a good thing. You've got no one to belay you, no one to help with the climbing. You're limited in what you can do.

In this situation you've got little option but to carefully traverse back and forth across the slope and try to get down to the Pillars of Haramon without breaking your neck.

What a disaster. Your first patrol and your cadets have rebelled, pushed you down the hill, and left you on your own, just because you didn't listen to them.

As you sit and ponder what to do, you remember what the officer said when you first started this trip, "you all have a vital part to play in the Slider Corps, and you need to listen to each other."

But you didn't listen. You thought you knew better. Your

ego made you lose the respect of your troop. You didn't work as a team.

You hang your head as you traverse back and forth across the slope on your way down. What will you say when you arrive alone? How will you explain?

You can only hope that you get another chance some day to make up for your mistake. That you get a chance to regain respect and become a valued member of the Highland Slider Corps.

This part of your story is over. Unfortunately you failed in your mission to get your troop to the Pillars of Haramon. However, you do have another chance. You can go back and try another path. Next time, listen to your fellow cadets.

It is time to make a decision. Do you want to:

Go to the very beginning of the story and try another path? **P1**

Or

Go to the list of choices and start reading from another part of the story? **P216**

You have decided to encourage the sliders to attack the Lowlanders.

You've heard stories about Lowland treachery all your life. You've never actually met a Lowlander, but you believe what your family says. "Miners, grab your picks and rope up," you yell to your team. "Get ready to fight."

As the sliders form themselves into a V-formation, ready to do a high-speed downhill attack, you and your fellow miners fit a light-weight cable drum to an anchor point in the rock ready to belay down and help. Once the cable is reeled out, each miner clips on to the line.

"We'll wait until the sliders attack, then we can reinforce where required," you tell the others.

The sliders are nearly ready to go. They sit on their utility belts with their feet forward, guide sticks tucked under their arms ready to steer. The Lowlanders know the effectiveness of this tactic and are retreating downhill around a small headland.

"On my mark!" the lead slider yells. "Three, two, one, go!"

You are amazed at how quickly the sliders gain speed as they rocket down the hillside. Each has their guide sticks pointing to the front ready to strike and their diamond studded boots up and ready to kick.

The sliders make a sweeping turn to the right. Within moments they too will be out of view.

"We need to move further down the valley so we can see

what's going on," you say to your group.

You push the release button on your zipper and slide down the cable past the protruding ridge to a point where you can see the sliders pursuing the retreating Lowlanders. The other miners follow your example.

Then you see a machine crawl out of a natural depression in the slope. It's an unusual contraption and surprisingly quick. It races up the valley towards the fleeing Lowlanders. When it reaches the retreating men, the machine stops and the Lowlanders climb in through a door in its armored side. Faces peer out tiny viewing holes along its side.

Mounted on the front of the machine is a high-speed drill which pecks holes in the ground. Behind the drill is a huge sprocket with pointed teeth.

The turning sprocket is powered by a chain that runs to a gear at the back where a vent releases steam and the thumping sound of an engine can be heard coming from within. As the sprocket turns, its teeth fit perfectly into the holes made by the drill, and pull it rapidly up the slope.

"I don't like this," you say to Piver. "What *is* that thing?"

For the first time ever, Piver looks serious. His cheeky grin is gone and his face is slack. "I don't know, but I doubt it's here to make our lives any easier."

The sliders have seen the machine too. They are doing their best to stop before they get too close. The high-pitched screech of dragging hooks echoes around the valley.

But the Lowlanders have planned their ambush well. The sliders are out in the open and have nowhere to hide. The machine blocks their downhill path. With a *twang*, a series of spring-loaded catapults, mounted on top of the machine, fling nets towards the now motionless sliders and because of their tight formation, the nets entangle many at once.

"This is not going well," Piver says

"We've got to go and help, but what can we do?" you say.

Before you and Piver have time to discuss the matter further, an amplified voice booms up the valley.

"Surrender now and you will be spared. This is your one and only warning."

Piver and the other miners look at you for instructions, their young faces showing their concern at the situation.

You never have liked ultimatums. "Quick, back to the sledges!" you yell. "Get aboard and cut them loose, we'll have to take our chances free sliding down the mountain."

Despite the look of fear on their faces, the other miners are quick to follow your lead. They zip back up the cable and rush to their respective sledges. Anchor lines are released and they jump aboard.

"Keep as high as you can, and head for the far side of the valley. We need to get out of here before the Lowlanders net us."

Each sledge has a simple steering system. Normally it is controlled by a slider at the front, but it can also be operated by a lever mounted on the side that is linked to the front runners. The diamond dust on the sledge's runners will give you some control, but any grip is reduced the faster you go.

"See those steep cliffs on the opposite side of the valley?"

You say. "Aim for those. We can use the slope below them to bank our turn and direct us back down the valley below the Lowlanders."

"Are you sure this is a good idea?" Piver asks. "It's going to be a pretty wild ride."

"Fancy life on a Lowland prison farm?" you reply.

Piver shakes his head.

"I didn't think so."

Having reeled in the sliders, the Lowland machine is grinding up the hill again. White steam belches and gears clunk.

"Let's go, we're running out of time!" You wave your arm for the other miners to follow and push off.

Your needle boots give you a little grip as you give the sledge a big shove and leap aboard. Before you know it you are gliding across the slope. Laying on your stomach, you grab the steering lever with your right hand while holding tightly onto a strap with your left. Your sledge cuts across the slope above the Lowlanders' machine and rockets towards the far cliffs, its runners clicking and clattering as they skitter across tiny ridges in the glassy black rock.

You hear the twang of nets being fired and the dull thud as they hit the slope behind you.

The speed of the free-running sledge is exhilarating and scary at the same time. You look back and see that the last sledge in your group has been snagged by a net and is being reeled in like a big fish. A day that had held such promise is quickly turning into a nightmare. Now there are only nine of you.

Normally, speed on the slopes is your enemy. Today however, it is your only chance to escape. How the Lowlanders got past the fortified Pillars of Haramon without being detected, you're not sure. What you do know is getting down the valley to the fortified base is your best chance. You certainly can't hang around on the slopes with this many Lowlanders around.

Your sledge slows as it begins to climb the slope on the far side of the valley. The cliffs are close now.

You pull the lever hard back to turn right and use the natural contour of the hill to bank your turn. The sledge swings around and you head back towards the opposite side of the valley at an angle that will take you well below the Lowlanders' position.

The valley has become a gigantic half-pipe as the sledges race down toward the Pillars. You swoop from one side to the other, using the natural banking to help you change direction and control your speed. A cool breeze whistles around your visor.

The machine is obviously better going uphill than down, because you've left it and the Lowlanders far behind.

After just over an hour of high-speed and at time crazy, on-the-edge sledging, you see two towering black columns rising from the valley floor. A distance that would have taken you and your slider escort a whole day to cover has been completed in hardly any time at all.

The massive Pillars of Haramon rise straight up from the

valley floor for over a thousand feet. They glisten in the afternoon light. At 100 yards wide, and perfectly smooth, apart from the numerous tunnels that pockmark their surface, the Pillars are one of the natural wonders of Petron.

Between the two monoliths are strung a number of sturdy cables with gondolas hanging beneath them so people and equipment can travel from one pillar to the other. Magnifying disks sit in some of the tunnel openings ready for use in case of attack.

A colony of pangos has made its home near the top of one of the pillars. These tasty but rather stupid birds provide a plentiful supply of fresh eggs and protein for the fort's occupants.

Although you can't see them from down below, you also know that some of the old mining tunnels are now used as hydro growing chambers and sleep pods for the three hundred or so Highlanders that make this isolated outpost their home.

As you steer onto the loading platform near the base of one of the pillars, a strong safety net catches your sledge and brings it to a halt. The rest of your group soon slides in to join you.

"Welcome to the Pillars of Haramon," says an officer that has come out of a portal to join you. "Where is your escort?"

After describing how your escort was captured by the Lowland machine and detailing your wild ride down the valley, the officer gets your group to park their sledges in a large chamber where cable drums, drills, grinders and other tools are stored.

"You must be exhausted after your ordeal," the office says, "but I'll need you to report this new information to Command right away. This is a serious development."

After your troop is directed to a visitor's pod where they can eat and rest, you follow the officer through a narrow portal and up a series of steps cut into the smooth black rock. Moon moths hang from the ceiling, lighting the way.

You crane your neck up so you can look at them as you walk.

"We encourage them to breed here. Saves us a lot of effort lighting all the tunnels," the officer says when he sees you studying the bright-winged creatures. "The Pillars have one of the biggest moth colonies on Petron."

You've never seen so many moon moth this close before. You are amazed by how their iridescent wings glow softly in the dark.

"They're beautiful," you say. "I'm surprised they aren't disturbed by your movement through the tunnels."

"Occasionally they'll get spooked and fly off all at once, but that's rare. I think they realize we mean them no harm."

Your leg muscles start to burn as you climb. Your breath is coming in gasps by the time you enter the command pod.

There are six officers in the pod. All but one gives you a quick once-over and then turn back to their work. The other comes over and directs you into a side chamber.

After repeating what you told the first officer about the

capture of your escort and the Lowland machine, the officer leans towards you. "So you've seen it. Do you think we can defeat this machine?"

You haven't really had much time to think about it. You and your fellow miners have been far too busy trying to stay alive on your crazy slide down the valley to have time to think about defeating the Lowland machine.

"Well?" the officer says.

"I … I'm not sure, sir. I'm a miner, not a slider."

"But you and your troop learned about engineering and mechanics in mining school. What is your honest opinion?"

You remember how easily the machine captured the sliders. How the drill on its front-end cut a track in the tough black rock allowing it to move quickly up the slope and how the machine's armor plating protected the Lowlanders within.

But then you remember the openings along the machine's side that allowed those within to see out, it's slower speed when moving downhill, and its reliance on an engine. You try to imagine how you would go about attacking such a contraption.

"Well…" You close your eyes and try to picture the machine. "If we can jam the drive gears the machine won't be able to move uphill," you say. "But can your sliders get close enough without being captured in their nets?"

The officer thinks hard for a moment and then nods slightly "Would you be willing to come with us? Sliders aren't trained mechanics. We aren't used to dealing with machinery. If you could come and tell us what we need to do to disable this thing, we'll find a way to get close enough somehow."

You want to help but you've not been trained for this sort of thing. You're a miner, not a tactician ... or a fighter for that matter. You know about drills and crystals and props and shafts. Maybe talking peace is the answer?

It seems to you that there are two possible solutions. Fight or talk.

There is a chance the Highlanders might be able to send the Lowland machine crashing back down the mountain. But do you want to be responsible if your plan doesn't work and it results in injury and death? Maybe talking peace with the Lowlanders is the best idea. Everyone loses something when it comes to war, even the victor.

It is time to make a decision. Do you:

Tell the officer you think they should talk peace with the Lowlanders? **P154**

Or

Volunteer to go with the sliders and attack the Lowland machine? **P157**

You have decided to yell out for the slider not to attack.

You stand up and move towards the head slider. "Hang on a minute! Aren't you going to find out what they want?"

The head slider looks at you and scowls. "They're Lowlanders. You expect me to trust them?"

"Do you see them carrying any weapons?" you say.

Squinting into the glare, the slider looks down at the Lowlanders again. He grumbles something under his breath, and then turns back to you. "Well I suppose we could hear what they have to say. But any tricky business and my troop will send them straight to the bottom!"

Piver gets up from behind his sledge and comes to stand beside you. He turns and whispers, "I'll come with you. Two heads are better than one, even if they are pango heads."

"You're crazy Piver, but I like your logic."

You take a step towards the head slider. "Piver and I will speak to them. I think it's better if your troop stays here. They'll feel less threatened that way."

The Lowlanders have stopped. They look up at you, their white flag fluttering.

"Well if you want to risk your lives, who am I to stop you?" the slider says.

You wonder if you really are risking your life. Maybe the head slider is right. Even though the Lowlanders are waving a white flag, have they really come in peace?

"Looks like the j—job is ours," Piver says nervously. "Do you want to do the talking or should I?"

"When we want to make them laugh, I'll let you know. In the mean time let me do the talking, okay?"

"We'd better throw down a line and go see what they want then." Piver takes a light-weight cable from his utility belt and ties one end onto an anchor bolt. Once it's attached, you both clip on and start working your way down the slope towards the Lowlanders.

When you and Piver are about five paces from the group you stop.

A couple of the Lowlanders look a little nervous. Not surprising considering there are thirty armed and highly trained sliders, arranged in attack formation, just waiting for an excuse to send them to the bottom.

"What are you doing way up here?" you ask, trying to keep your voice from wavering. "You're a long way from home, don't you think?"

One of the Lowlanders takes a step forward and pulls out a small tablet. He unfolds its protective cover and starts to read. "I come as a representative of the Lowland Council. My council wishes to meet with your Highland leaders to see if we can find a way to end the bloodshed that has plagued our two peoples for so many years. In exchange for peace, all the Lowland Council requires is a small act of good faith on behalf of the Highlanders."

"Act of good faith?"

"A small tax, to cover the cost of administration, health and education," he continues. You will gain many benefits from becoming part of the Federation of Lowland States."

"What do you consider small?"

"A mere ten percent of any minerals mined from the Black Slopes. A very reasonable request, don't you think? You pay nearly that much to the border traders already in commission, not to mention what it must cost you to defend the Highlands."

You shrug. His proposal doesn't sound unreasonable. Some education you already get, but there are only limited health facilities in the Highlands.

You look briefly at Piver, shrug, and then turn back to the Lowland leader. "I'm happy to pass your message on to my superiors. How do we contact you with our answer?"

"We have troops gathered in the foothills below the Pillars of Haramon. Tell your leaders to send an envoy to us there with your answer no later than the last day of the full moon. If we don't hear from you by then…"

You wait for him to finish his sentence but he remains silent.

"Then what?" you ask.

"Let's just say if I were in your position, I'd do my best to persuade my leaders to do as we suggest. Believe me when I say your Highland sliders are no match for our recently developed technology. The Highland communities can either choose to be a small part of our federation or we will send you all to the bottom. It's your choice."

With that, the Lowlanders turn and move off down the hill.

You press the trigger on the handle of your zipper, its

battery whirs and pulls you up the cable where the others have been waiting.

The head slider shuffles over. "Well, what did they say?"

You give him the main points of the discussion.

"Those ... those Lowland scum," the lead slider says. "We should send them back to their leaders in pieces. How dare they demand such a thing!"

"Wait," Piver says. "The Highland Council should be the ones to decide."

You nod your head. "Piver's right. It's not our place to start a war. Besides, their offer could be of some benefit."

The head slider is almost growling in disgust. "I think we should attack while we have the numerical advantage. Then there will be less Lowlanders to fight later. But seeing you miners are paying for our escort to the Pillars..."

You understand the slider's position. Hatred of Lowlanders runs deep in the Slider Corps, but you also know that war is a costly exercise, even for the winner.

The situation is tense. It is time for you to make a decision. Do you:

Join the sliders and attack the Lowlanders? **P141**

Or

Carry on to the Pillars of Haramon with the Lowlanders' message? **P198**

You have decided to tell the officer you think they should talk peace with the Lowlanders.

"Look," you say to the slider officer, "I don't know how to disable the Lowlanders' machine. What if my ideas fail? Surely talking peace is a better option, especially when the opposition has a technological advantage."

The officer sneers at you like you're a pango dropping he needs to scrape off his boot. "If you won't help, I'm sure one of the other miners will come up with a plan."

"But…"

The officer's face is turning red. "Sliders do not surrender. We attack!" he yells. "I should have known better than to ask a miner for help."

You can't understand the officer's reaction. When did you say anything about surrender? Talking and compromising isn't surrender, it's saving lives.

"Wait, I didn't say surrender…"

But the officer isn't listening. He has stomped away and is talking with a stern-faced officer on the far side of the pod. You can tell you'd be wasting your breath trying to reason with him anymore. He stopped listening the moment you said "peace".

After being ignored for a few minutes, you realize you may as well head back to the other miners. Besides, you're not a slider, and therefore not under slider control. You and your fellow miners can make up your own minds about the situation.

When you re-enter the pod, the miners look at you expectantly.

"What's going on?" one of them says.

"Yeah," says Piver. "Has war been declared?"

"It's certainly looking that way," you say. "These sliders aren't keen on talking."

"What should we do?" Piver asks.

"We need to make a decision. We either help Slider Command or leave the Pillars and make our way back up the mountain to home. If there is going to be an invasion I know where I want to be and that's with my family."

You look at the worried faces all around you.

"But how will we get home?" one of the miners says.

Piver is looking increasingly agitated, but he comes and stands by your side.

You glance around, trying to gauge the mood of the others. "We can leave the mining equipment here and make our way back home by using the tows and the safe routes."

Miners are shaking their heads and mumbling under their breath. Most come from a long line of mining families. The idea of striking out across the slopes without a slider escort is unthinkable. They are far less informed about travel on the slopes. Understandably it frightens them.

You may not be a trained slider, but you've heard slider stories and discussions on tactics and tricks for maneuvering on black glass ever since you were a baby. Mining school taught you a few trick about getting around as well. With a bit of gear from your sledge, you're confident you can get back home without an escort.

From the body language, and mumblings of the miners, you can tell they want to stay where they are, safe under the protection of the base commander here at the Pillars of Haramon.

But you're not sure about that man. He seems a little too eager to fight. You were always taught to think for yourself rather than blindly follow orders that don't seem right. On the other hand, you can't deny that travelling the slopes can be dangerous, and you don't like the idea of leaving your classmates behind.

It is time to choose. Do you:

Help Command disable the Lowland machine? **P157**

Or

Leave the Pillars of Haramon and strike out for home on your own? **P169**

You have decided to volunteer to go with the sliders and attack the Lowland machine.

You can't bring yourself to leave your comrades, so helping Slider Command seems your only option. The Lowlanders and their strange machine will create havoc amongst the Highland communities if something isn't done quickly. You'll most likely end up fighting anyway, so you may as well do it before the Lowlanders are any higher up the mountain.

Your family would be disappointed if they found out you hadn't volunteered. If things go wrong, at least you would have tried to make a difference. You let your fellow miners know what you intend and go back to the stairs and start climbing.

"The miners will help," you tell the officer in the command pod. "We all have mechanical knowledge, but only myself and Piver come from slider families and know how to move safely around the slopes. The others should stay here to help fortify the Pillars."

"That makes sense," the office says with a curt nod. "The last thing I want is a bunch of miners slowing us down." The officer holds out his hand. "Welcome to the mission. Glad you've decided to come along."

As you shake the officer's hand, you wonder if you've made the right decision. You've been on a few trips around the Highlands with your family and they've taught you a few basics about travelling around the slopes, but your experience is limited. You might know more than the other miners in your group, but compared to these sliders, you're only a beginner.

"Go get your equipment. Make sure you and Piver are at the main portal in twenty minutes," the officer says. "Pack as light as you can. We'll be moving fast."

You start back down the steps towards the accommodation pod, but before you get far, a faint voice echoes down the staircase. You stop to listen.

"You really think two miners are going to make any difference? They're not much more than kids."

"What other option do we have?" the officer says. "Their mechanical knowledge is our last hope. How many people did we lose trying to stop that machine from skirting around our defenses?"

The unfamiliar voice does not reply.

The conversation fades as it moves to another part of the command pod and all you can hear are mumbles.

Maybe the outspoken Highlander was right. Maybe you won't be much use stopping the machine. All that you know is that you have to try.

When you get back to the others, you pull Piver aside and tell him the plan.

"We're going with the sliders?" Piver says. "Geebus! Thanks for asking me!"

You give Piver a little grin. "The sliders seemed a bit glum. I thought you could cheer them up a little."

"Funny ha ha," Piver says. "I doubt there will be much to

joke about when we're all free sliding towards the bottom."

The two of you head down to your sledges.

"I think tangling their machine in cables somehow, is our only chance to stop it," you say to Piver as you work. "It shouldn't take much to jam up all those gears and chains."

"Assuming they don't net us before we get close enough."

Piver is right. Your slider escort didn't do too well. Why should this lot fare any better?

Between the two of you, you sort out what you need from the sledges. It isn't much because you have to carry whatever you take. You pack a launcher with some spare charges, an impact drill, and an assortment of hand tools, cables, zippers and clips.

Piver grabs a spool of high-temp cutting cord as well. "I've always wanted to use this stuff!" he says. "I hear it cuts through rock at over a foot a second."

"Just don't drop it. I've also heard it's not that stable."

You hear movement behind you as a troop of sliders make their way down one of the tunnels towards the portal. The sliders tower over you and the even smaller Piver. Their uniforms show off their muscular legs and arms. Each has a pack on their backs and a utility belt around their waists.

The officer from earlier is among them. "You miners ready?"

You swallow and nod.

He throws you each a pair of diamond spurs. "Better put these on. Should keep you from slipping."

The diamonds on the spurs are tiny, but each is cut in

such a way that a sharp point digs into the rock every time you dig in your heel.

Once strapped onto your boots, you try them out. The grip they provide is remarkable. Then to your amazement he hands you a guide stick.

"You'll need one of these too," the office says. "Look after it, they're expensive to replace."

You look at the stick in your hand. "Wow, thanks. I never thought I'd get to use one of these."

"Pretty hard to travel with the Highland Slider Corps without one," the office says. "Just remember it's a lot more sensitive than the cheap commercial models so don't over correct on your turns."

Without further ceremony, the officer pulls a lever just inside the portal and a section of the wall rolls back to reveal a steeply angled tunnel disappearing down into the ground.

One of the Highland sliders sits on the ground next to the hole and lowers his feet into it. Then without warning he pushes off and disappears with a *whoosh*.

"Where's he going?" you ask the officer.

"This shaft takes us below ground to a secret chamber," the officer says. "When the miners first started excavating here at the Pillars of Haramon, they had to figure out a way to get rid of all the excess rock. To solve the problem, they drilled a tunnel from under the Pillars, up through the hillside to the ridge above. Inside this tunnel, they built a high-speed conveyor that took the rubble up and dumped it into the valley on the other side where it slid down the hill and into a crevasse."

"Sounds like a lot of work," you say.

"It was, but the rich pickings made it all worthwhile. Fifty years ago, when the main mining operation ceased, the Slider Corps began using the conveyor as a lift to get troops up the mountain where we have the advantage of altitude over any invaders. Sure beats climbing or using tows. Besides, a conventional tow would be vulnerable to attack. This one is totally hidden."

"Why haven't I heard about this?" you ask the officer.

"It's ultra-top-secret."

"Great." Piver said with a grin. "Now that we know their secret, they'll have to kill us."

The officer looks down at Piver, shakes his head and chuckles. "Only if the Lowlanders don't get you first."

The two of you watch slider after slider drop feet first into the tunnel. When it is your turn you sit on the ground and scoot nervously towards the edge. All you can see is the first fifteen feet of smooth black rock angling steeply down into the darkness. You hesitate…

"Happy landing," the officer says pushing you towards the edge with the toe of his boot. "Don't forget to bend your knees."

"Wait I'm not… Whoa!" You feel your stomach lurch for a second or so, but then the tunnel gently angles you down into the core of the mountain. It feels strange sliding in complete darkness. The turns and twist are so frequent, at times it's hard to tell up from down.

When a faint light reflects off the stone in the distance, you know you'd better relax and get ready for impact. With a *swish* you pop out of the tunnel into a wide chamber. Moon moths cluster together on the ceiling, giving you enough light to see sliders standing around waiting for the rest of you to arrive.

You skid across the floor and come to rest in a fine net stretched across the chamber. Strong hands pull you to your feet.

"Wow, that was strange," you say. "Sliding in the darkness is really disorientating."

"You get used to it," a slider says.

You hear a delighted squeal as Piver pops out of the tunnel. "Geebus that was fun! Forget this mining lark. I want to be a slider!"

Piver throws his head back and laughs with his mouth open so wide you could drop a pango egg down his throat without even touching the sides. You've never seen him so animated.

"Pleased you enjoyed it," the officer says. "Now will you stop giggling like an idiot and get ready to move out."

Piver snaps his mouth shut, turns bright red and adjusts his pack.

While you sort your gear, the officer walks across the chamber towards a wide belt whirring up another tunnel. Every ten feet or so, a metal lip runs across the width of the belt. These barriers would have stopped the crushed rock from sliding back down the belt as it travelled to the surface for disposal.

"This next part is tricky," the office says. "You've got to time your jump so you end up on a flat part of the conveyor. Those metal shutters are hard and the belt is moving at pace so be careful. If you keep low and lean forward, you'll be fine."

You watch the sliders time their jump as you move towards the front of the line. The large drum that is rotating the belt beneath your feet makes the floor of the chamber vibrate.

"I'll count you in," the officer says.

You move to the edge of the conveyor and prepare to jump.

"On my mark. Three, two, one, now."

You hit the belt and immediately drop to all fours. The belt is really moving. Before long you are in total darkness once again.

"Don't worry," the slider behind you says. "Getting off is the easy part."

When you get to the top you see why. The belt dives around another drum, and deposits you into a narrow chute that slopes down towards a drop-off some twenty yards away. All you can see at the end of the chute is … nothing!

"Whoa!" you yell, as you scrabble for something to hold on to. But there is nothing but smooth black glass.

You only see the ultra-fine netting strung up across the chute, as it brings you to a sudden stop a yard from the edge of the cliff.

"Phew." You say as you regain your feet. "You should warn people about that. I thought I was heading to the bottom."

You see the sliders trying to suppress their laughter. It's obviously a trick they play on everyone who takes the conveyor for the first time.

When you hear a squeal of abject terror behind you, you know Piver has arrived.

"Geebus!" Piver says as he wobbles over to join you. "I nearly pooped myself."

A few of the sliders hear Piver's comments and laugh.

"Tell me about it!" you say to Piver. "Seems you're not the only comedian on this trip."

The officer taps his guide stick on the ground. "Okay, listen up people. We've got an important mission to accomplish. We need to figure out how to stop this new weapon the Lowlanders have developed. We've brought two miners with us for their mechanical expertise. Look after them. We need them in one piece."

"I like being in one piece," Piver whispers.

You tap him in the shin with the toe of your boot. "Shush."

"Ouch." Piver bends down and rubs his leg. No need to kick me.

Then you see the smirk on his face.

The officer continues. "We're going to traverse along this ridge as far as we can. Hopefully the Lowlanders are still in the valley. Once we find them, we'll assess the situation and then decide what to do."

"You miners will be linked to a slider front and back. If you feel yourself beginning to fall, yell out immediately so my men have time to put in an emergency belay. Got it?"

The two of you nod. This is all beginning to sound rather serious.

"Parts of this ridge have been overrun by morph rats, so watch out for burrows," the officer says. "We don't want anyone breaking a leg."

"Just what we need, morph rats," Piver says. "Those things give me the creeps."

You're not a big fan of morph rats either. They eat everything in their path and they leave burrows in the most unexpected places. You also hate the sticky slime that covers their hairless bodies, and the sucking sound their feet make as they move around the slopes.

You've heard they're edible, but by the time all the slime and stench is boiled off them, and their tough hide is removed, the small amount of stringy meat you'd get seems hardly worth the effort.

The officer is speaking again. "… okay, let's get our boots locked and get ready to move out. We need to take advantage of what light we have left."

Everyone clips their boots together and shuffles into a line. The officer is out front and will lead the troop himself.

"On my count. Three, two, one…"

He pushes off and starts traversing across the slope along a narrow path worn into its surface. The path runs ever so slightly downhill, but because the ridge is high above the valley floor, you are still able to travel up towards its head. By the time you reach the valley floor, your group is already three or four miles above the Pillars.

"We'll have to use zip lines from here," the office says.

You pull your scope from your pocket and scan the upper slopes. Everything is dark and in shadow. There is no sign of the Lowlanders or their machine.

The officer turns to you and Piver. "Can you fire an anchor bolt into that pinnacle up there?" He points up the slope to where an old volcanic pipe rises out of the slope near the ridgeline. "We could zip up and continue traversing that way. Save our legs for when we find the Lowlanders."

You waste no time in setting up the launcher. Climbing has never been your strong point.

When the launcher is ready to go, Piver sets off the charge.

The anchor bolt streaks off with a hiss towards its target as the fine cable whirls off the drum beside you.

"Whoa, look at it go!" Piver says.

With a cloud of dust, the bolt smacks into the rock at the base of the pinnacle.

"Nice shot," the officer says. "Okay. Let's get up there and get sliding."

Once you're on the ridge, having gained some valuable altitude, you pull out your scope again. The machine is hard to spot in the shadows of the upper slope, but its tiny puffs of steam give its position away.

"I see them," you say. "They're at twenty-eight degrees, south by southeast."

The officer pulls out his scope and checks the coordinates. "Good spotting. Looks like they're getting their camp sorted before dewfall. We need to get above them if we're to have any chance of sending them to the bottom."

You go back to your scope and watch the Lowlanders' preparations. You can just barely make out the track their machine has made as it drilled its way up the hillside. The Lowlanders have anchored it on a semi-flat spur near a side gully.

Some of the Lowlanders are rigging up covers in case it rains, while others are tending cooking pots.

You can see Lowland guards stationed on the upper side of the machine. If an attack is to come, they know the Highlanders are most likely to strike from above.

Meanwhile the sliders are talking about climbing around the Lowlanders so they can attack from above in typical slider style. This makes you think.

You zoom in on the track and see the regular series of holes the machine has drilled into the slope. This track runs all the way up the valley like a staircase.

If the Lowlanders are expecting an attack from above, why not use the track made by their own machine to climb up and attack at night after dewfall when the Lowlanders least expect it?

But what happens if the Lowlanders spot you coming? You will be below them and they will have the advantage of altitude. Your suggestion could be responsible for a terrible defeat.

It is time to make a decision. Do you?

Suggest an attack from below? **P183**

Or

Stay quiet, let the sliders plan an attack from above? **P190**

You have decided to leave the Pillars and strike out for home.

You put your hands on your hips and look at the other miners. "Well I don't know about you lot, but I'm not going to get involved in a war without at least trying to find a peaceful solution. If you want to follow some blood-crazed slider, be my guest!"

As you start packing up your gear, everyone mills about not knowing what to do.

"In fact, you probably should stay here," you say, as you shoulder your pack. "I don't need a bunch of inexperienced miners slowing me down."

You leave the pod and head towards the sledges to get the extra gear you'll need to make the long trip back to your home community.

After untying the cover on your sledge you grab a spool of light-weight cable, an extra zipper, some anchors and a cable launcher and stow them in your pack along with some travel rations and broth. Then you sit to strap on the pair of diamond spurs your family gave you as a going away present. "In case you ever need grip in a hurry," they'd said.

Just as you are tightening the last strap, you hear footsteps coming down the corridor. It's Piver.

"Didn't think I'd let you go on your own did you?"

You give him a big smile and slap him affectionately on the back. "I was hoping you'd decide to come," you say as he starts packing. "It's a lot safer moving around the slopes with two. That's for sure."

After ten minutes or so, you've both got everything sorted. Then Piver starts strapping on some spurs.

"I see you got a going away present too," you say.

"Slider parents are like that," Piver says. "Just as well, eh?"

"Yup, just as well."

"Should we tell the sliders we're leaving?" Piver asks.

"Don't worry, they'll see us. Let's just hope that crazy slider in charge doesn't go completely mental and try to fry us with one of their big magnifying lens."

Piver's eyes widen. "Would he do that?"

"Don't worry, it will only hurt for a minute,"

Piver's face goes white.

"Got you!"

Piver exhales with a rush of air. "That wasn't funny."

You chuckle and lift your pack onto your shoulders and tighten the waist strap. "Shall we start climbing?"

Without looking at Piver, you head towards the portal. You're pleased when you hear the distinctive click of diamond spurs behind you.

It's just as well you've studied this area. There are a number of routes you can take, but because dewfall isn't that far away, you and Piver will need to find a safe place to camp for the night within a couple hours.

"Let's launch a cable up to the ridge and gain some altitude," you tell Piver. "We need to get sliding if we're to make any distance."

The two of you put a charge in the launcher's tube and fire a light cable up to a rocky outcrop on the hillside above you. There is a puff of black dust as the anchor bolt buries itself into the rock.

"Up we go," you say as you clip your zipper onto the cable. "See you at the top."

The charge in the zipper is good for three thousand vertical feet. After that, you'll have to do your climbing the hard way.

Once the two of you reach the top, you look back at the Pillars below. "Beautiful, aren't they?"

Piver is deep in thought and doesn't reply.

Far below, low cloud is banking up against the foothills. The Borderlands are disappearing into the mist, which make the Black Slopes look like an island set in a violent sea of purple foam and crashing waves.

Over the next two hours, you and Piver make good distance by zipping up and then traversing. You are pleased you paid attention in navigation class when the entrance of an abandoned mine appears right where you calculated it would be.

"Looks like we've got shelter for the night," Piver says.

"As long as the morph rats haven't taken over." The thought of the slimy creatures gives you the shivers.

"Should I toss a screecher in?" Piver asks "That'll flush them out."

"Good thinking, but I didn't bring any."

"Just as well I did then." Piver unclips a round object

from his belt and pushes a button on one end. A high-pitched ear-splitting screech starts to blast out.

"Quick toss it!" you yell, clamping your hands to the side of your head.

Piver throws the sphere into the opening of the mine shaft and steps to one side. You do the same. If there are morph rats in the hole, it won't be long before they scurry out.

As the two of you stand with your backs to the stone wall on either side of the shaft's entrance, you hear the screecher rolling further down the tunnel.

At first the clicking is faint, but before long its volume increases. Morph rats are coming. Within a minute it sounds like a thousand pebbles are bouncing along the tunnel towards you. The first morph rat scuttles past and throws itself out of the opening and slurps and slimes its way down the slope. More follow in a slithering mass of hairless bodies.

The rats don't notice the two of you in their headlong rush to get away from the brain piercing sound that is amplified by their extremely good sense of hearing and the hollowness of the tunnel. It smells like the tunnel has farted as the rats pass.

"Geebus that's horrible!" Piver says holding his nose.

You look over at him and can't help but laugh at his expression. "You should have stood on the upwind side of the opening."

'Piver clutches his throat and screws up his face, playing it up for all he's worth. By the time the last morph rat has disappeared, the two of you are on your hands and knees laughing.

You give the stench a moment to clear and then enter the tunnel, careful to walk on the high side of the tunnel, away from the puddles of slime left behind by the departing rats.

While you set up a small burner to heat some broth, Piver rummages in his pack for some hydro bars. Once camp is sorted you sit down around the burner and eat.

Piver takes a sip of broth and then looks up. "So what are you going to do when you get home?"

"I'm not really sure. Try to talk the communities into making peace with the Lowlanders I think. It's time we try to work things out between us. Surely we have more in common than differences. Who benefits from war?"

Piver takes another sip and nods his head. "Makes sense."

Then you hear the sound of footsteps at the mine's opening. Who could that be?

You and Piver look up from your food.

"Hello traitors!" a gruff voice says. "We thought you might stay here for the night."

You recognize one of the men from the command pod. It's the slider the officer was talking to after you told him you thought they should talk peace with the Lowlanders.

"What are you doing here?" you ask. "And what do you mean, traitors?"

"You didn't think Slider Command was going to let you walk away did you? Stupid miners!"

You don't like the sound of this. What is he inferring? Are they going to take you back to the Pillars?

"Yeah, stupid miners," the other slider says. "Time you had an accident and went for a slide."

The two sliders look at you and Piver. It sounds like they're planning to throw you down the slope.

"But it's after dewfall." you say. "We'll go all the way to the bottom."

"Not our problem," the officer says. "We've been listening to your conversation and know you're off to spread discontent amongst the communities. That doesn't suit Slider Command."

"Peace doesn't suit Slider Command?" you ask the officer. "Are you afraid you'll lose all your power and influence?"

"So naïve," the officer grunts.

The two sliders turn and have a brief conversation. While they do, you catch Piver's eye and nod towards the slime trail running down one side of the tunnel where the morph rats ran out. It's a slippery mess, but it might be your only chance.

"Time for a slide all right," you say to the men as you snag your pack and launch yourself, belly first, onto the trail of slime heading down into the depths of the tunnel.

You hear a grunt as Piver hits the slope behind you.

You spin around onto your back and place your feet below you, hoping they will protect you if you run into anything unexpected.

"Whoaaaa!" you hear Piver say behind you. "Where does this go?"

His voice sounds frightened, and so he should be. But at least this way, you are sure the sliders won't follow you.

"Stay loose and get ready for a sudden stop," you yell back to Piver. "If I remember the map correctly, there's a side tunnel coming up that leads to an exit further down."

Your speed is increasing as you slide through the darkness. The slime smells of rat and feels both sticky and slippery at the same time.

"I feel I'm sliding through liquid fart," Piver yells. "Death might be better than this!"

No way are you opening your mouth to reply.

Your momentum is slowed as you splash into the pool of slime at the bottom of the tunnel. Before you know it, you are sitting waist-deep in the awful stuff.

Faint moonlight reaches you from a tunnel opening to your right.

"Ewwww!" Piver say, lifting his arms above the slimy mess. "This stuff is worse than pango poo!"

"Better than going to the bottom though don't you think?"

"Only just," Piver says as he stands up and struggles out of the sticky muck.

The two of you use your hands to sweep the slime off your torso and legs. Thankfully your uniforms are made from a tightly woven water repellant fabric that comes clean relatively easily.

"I don't hear anything from above," Piver says, tilting his head. "What now?"

"Don't worry, I have a plan."

"I hope it's better than diving into a stinking pool of slime," Piver says.

"If only it were that simple," you say with a smile. "Did your family ever tell you the story of the back-to-back slide made by two slider cadets when the Black Slopes were first being settled?"

"They got caught in a storm, didn't they?"

"That's right. They had no option but to abandon their camp after six days and take their chances free sliding. They sat on their packs and linked arms back to back. Then, using only spurs to steer, they took off down the mountain."

"I remember," Piver said. "But…"

"Remember how the rear cadet dragged his spurs like an anchor to slow them down, and the front cadet used his to steer?"

"So that's your plan? A suicide slide back to the Pillars?"

"Not to the Pillars, to the Lowlands!"

"All the way to the bottom? Geebus, are you crazy?" Piver's eyes search your face. "You're serious, aren't you?"

"We have to talk to the Lowlanders and get them to hold off any invasion until we have time to speak to the elders in the communities. We need to end the conflict once and for all."

You can see Piver's mind working. He shakes his head and mumbles something under his breath. Then he looks up at you and smiles. "You always said I was crazy. Now it looks like I get a chance to prove you right."

You slap Piver on the back. "Good. Now try to get some sleep. We'll take off at first light."

The next morning, after a quick bite, you move over to the exit and pull a map out of the pouch on your belt. Unfolding it, you lay the map out on the floor in the dim light and study the contours of the terrain you will be sliding over.

"It will be plain sliding until we reach the Pillars. If we stay in the shadow, on the left of Long Gully, we should slip right past without anyone noticing."

"But not too far left," Piver says, jabbing his finger at the map. "Or we'll end up in the crevasse field."

You nod in agreement. "It's the ridges below the Pillars that scare me." You point out an area of rough ground that looks extremely dangerous.

"The words slice and dice come to mind," Piver says. "I've seen pictures of what happens to people who hit riffle ridges at speed. It's not pretty."

Your finger traces a narrow valley that branches off Long Gulley just below the Pillars. "That's why we need to take this route. It's the only safe way to the bottom."

Piver's eyebrows crease as he studies the map. "You think we'll find it sliding at speed?"

"We'd better."

The two of you sit at the tunnel's exit, your feet dangling over the edge. You realize there is every chance that this could be the last sunrise you ever see. For some reason, as the sun peeks over the mountains in the distances, this thought makes the scene even more beautiful.

When the light reaches the slopes below you, you turn to Piver. "We'd better get going."

Piver nods and follows your lead by creating a seat from his backpack. He tightens the arm straps around his legs to hold it firmly in place.

It may not be much, but at least the packs will give you some protection from the friction and bumps as the two of you slide down the hillside.

"Now make sure you keep even pressure on both of your spurs unless I yell left or right. If I do, just drag that spur until I say release. Got it?"

Piver gulps. "I think so."

After some final adjustment to your straps, you both scoot towards the edge. With Piver's back against yours, the two of you lock your arms together and stretch out your legs testing the bite of your spurs.

"Ready Piver?"

"It's all downhill from here," he replies, giving a shove that sends you both over the edge and onto the steep slope below.

Before you know it, you are moving with pace towards the valley floor. Piver's heels screech like a pair of demented pangos behind you, sending a shiver down your spine. A quarter mile down the valley you make a sweeping turn. Up to your right, you see the two sliders standing on the ridge.

They are shaking their heads.

"Yippee!" Piver yells at the top of his voice. "Try to catch us now, morph heads!"

You admire Piver's spirit, but you also know the sliders have no intention of following. Why would they? They think you're sliding to the bottom, and not in a good way. And maybe they're right. They certainly will be if you miss the entrance to the side valley you hope to take.

"Left!" you yell when you see a small crevasse in the slope below you. "Left!"

The screech of Piver's spur increases as he digs it in. You kick your right boot into the slope at the same time, shunting the two of you further to the left. You skid past the crack with barely a yard to spare.

"Whoa, that was close," Piver says looking back up the slope.

"Release!"

Piver goes back to dragging both heels equally.

You see the Pillars looming up in the distance. "Left!" you yell again. "Pillars coming up. "

Surely guards at the Pillars will hear your spurs as you slide past. Thankfully the sun isn't high enough for Slider Command to be able to use their burning lens yet. Otherwise the two of you would be toast.

Despite Piver dragging his spurs for all he's worth, the remaining dampness on the glassy black rock means you are sliding fast. The speed makes you wonder if you'll have enough control to enter the narrow valley.

"Hard left!" you yell. "I see the entrance!"

Both of you use your heels desperately trying to move left on the slope. You stab your right heel down in repeated motions. With each kick you move a yard to the left.

"Harder!" you yell to Piver.

You kick your heel into the slope, bang, bang, bang as fast as you can. Then you're in.

"Release!" You let out a breath. "Phew, that was scary."

"Imagine what it's like when you're sliding backwards." Piver says, with a slight tremor in his voice.

The sun is up over the ridge now and is starting to reach the valley floor. Within a few miles, your progress slows a little as you hit drier slopes. You feel your control growing.

"I think we're actually going to make it," you say with relief.

The slopes begin to flatten out and within another ten minutes you are barely moving.

"I can see the Lowland camp," you tell Piver.

"Let's just hope they're as pleased to see us as we are to see them."

You dig your heels in and slide to a stop just as the last of the black rock disappears under a slope covered in pale green moss. The two of you stand and stretch your backs and shoulders.

As you stretch, you look around. It seems strange to see so much flat land in front of you. "It's so lush," you say.

Piver studies the scene. "Yeah … weird isn't it. But it's pretty in a funny sort of way."

You can't help but agree. You adjust your pack and look towards the Lowlanders' camp. "I suppose we'd better go talk to them."

"Can I do the greeting?" Piver asks. "I've got a phrase in mind that I've always wanted the opportunity to use."

"Oh yeah? And what's that?"

"Take me to your leader," Piver says with a chuckle.

You shake your head. "You really are nuts you know."

"For once I'm pleased to say I'm not the only one."

As the two of you walk towards the Lowland camp, you wonder if you'll be okay. Will the Lowlanders be friendly?

You're apprehension doesn't last long. Before you get to the cluster of Lowland huts a group of children run out to greet you. As they crowd around, one holds out a crackle berry, the legendary fruit of the Lowlands.

You've heard stories about this celebrated fruit. You've even seen a picture of it in one of your school books. But no one from the Highlands has seen one up close, let alone tasted one, for over 300 years since the fighting began.

While you're thinking about this offering, Piver snatches the crackle berry and sinks his teeth into its succulent blue flesh.

You watch and wait, wondering if he'll like it.

As Piver chews, and without even realizing it, he rises up onto his toes and does a little jiggle with his hips. Then he sinks back down, wipes his lips with the back of his hand and says, "Geebus! That's the best thing I've ever tasted!"

Congratulations, you made it down the mountain in one piece and are about to start talks that might bring about peace between the Highlanders and the Lowlanders. Well done! But have you tried all the different paths the story takes?

You now have one more decision to make. Do you:

Go back to the very beginning of the story and try another path? **P1**

Or

Go to the list of choices and start reading from another part of the story? **P216**

You have decided to suggest an attack from below.

You put down your scope and take a step towards the officer. "I think we might have a better chance if we sneak up from below."

The officer gives you a funny look. "What? Are you mad?"

You know your suggestion goes against every slider principle. All your life you've heard about the advantage of altitude, but maybe new times need new solutions.

"Look," you say, pointing towards the series of holes running up the valley. "The Lowlanders have provided us with a staircase that leads right to their camp. We can climb at night after dewfall. They'll never expect us."

You can see the cogs in the officer's mind working. His brow scrunches together and he scratches the side of his face. He pulls out his scope and looks again at the track. Then he calls one of his men over and has a chat.

After a moment, he turns back to you. "Okay so let's say we go along with your pango-brained scheme. What do we do once we're in the camp?"

"We mount a winch further down the mountain. Once we get to the Lowlanders' camp, we hook a cable onto their machine, cut its anchors, and winch the thing off the mountain. Once the machine is dislodged from its track, it will only have one way to go."

"Can you guarantee your equipment can pull that machine out of its track?"

You nod. "We can if you and your sliders can keep the Lowlanders off our back long enough."

Piver nods his agreement. "That machine will go all the way to the bottom and believe me, it won't be in very good order once it gets there."

"May our ancestors have mercy on us," the officer says. "If this fails, we'll go down in history as the sliders who attacked from below. I hope you're prepared to become a laughing stock."

"Or heroes," you say.

With the decision made to climb the machine's track after dark, your group moves to a safe spot to wait for dewfall. Then once it's dark, the long climb up to the Lowlanders' camp can begin.

The spot the sliders have chosen to wait is tucked into a shallow depression about a mile below the Lowlanders' camp. With all the shadow in the valley, the dark colors of your uniforms will blend in with the slope.

Everyone moves carefully. Noises travel a long way in the still evening air and you don't want to alert the Lowlanders of your presence. Only the distant screech of pangos and the sound of activity in the Lowland camp break the silence.

The waiting sliders are all clipped onto a strong cable. Some eat dried hydro while they await the order to climb.

About an hour after dark the officer whispers for everyone to prepare to move out. It will be a slow climb due to the need for quiet and the dampness of the rock. Anything that can clunk or clang is secured into pockets.

Your pack is heavy and awkward.

"Move out," the officer signals with his hand.

You slot your toes and fists into the holes bored by the machine and take a step up. Shifting you hands to the next set of holes, you repeat the motion until you and the sliders have established a rhythm. The weight of your gear wants to pull you back so you make sure to keep your weight forward on the steep slope.

When your group is about 100 yards below the Lowland camp, you and Piver use a couple of expansion bolts to lock the winch into the track holes. Piver attaches a heavy-duty cable to the winch's drum and hands the spool to one of the sliders to carry the rest of the way up.

Leaving Piver below, you and the sliders start to climb again. It will be your responsibility to connect the cable to the Lowland machine in such a way that it does not snap when the winch is activated. The sliders will cut the machine's tethers and keep the Lowlanders busy.

Despite the cold night, sweat drips from your forehead. You're not used to this sort of exercise.

The leading sliders have reached the camp. You can see their shadowy figures moving around just below the machine. Through a series of hand signals, you are instructed to move forward. A slider hands you the end of the cable and you start looking for the best possible place to attach it to the machine.

It's important that the cable twists the machine sideway so it dislodges the sprocket from the holes in the track. If it only pulls straight down, the winch may not have enough power.

You look at the sides of the machine, but they are smooth. There is no obvious protrusion for the cable to hook on to. Then you see a bracket that forms part of the catapult mechanism. It looks a perfect place to attach the cable, but it's above your reach along the top edge of the machine.

You signal the slider beside you and point to the bracket. He nods, understanding your problem. Interlacing his fingers he creates a place to put your foot and hoists you up so that you can hook the shackle onto the bracket.

You've just finished securing the shackle when there is a shout from the camp.

The Lowland guards have spotted someone and raised the alarm.

"Down the cable!" you yell to the Highlanders.

The Highlander lowers you to the ground and the two of you clip on to the cable.

"Quickly."

Going down is a lot easier than going up. All you have to do is pull a trigger on your zipper and you slide freely down the cable. Release the trigger and the zipper clamps onto the cable and brings you to a halt.

Before you know it you and the Highlanders are back beside Piver.

"Now, Piver. Let's rip that scab off the mountain!"

Piver wastes no time in throwing the winch into gear. It

splutters and coughs, then starts to wind the excess cable around the drum. By the time all the slack cable is wound up the drum is spinning at quite a good speed.

You hold your breath. Will it be strong enough to jerk the machine off the hillside?

When the last of the slack has been taken up, the cable rises off the ground and starts to stretch.

Any moment now.

"I don't know if it's going to be strong enough," Piver says as the winch groans in protest.

Then you hear yelling from up the mountainside. Lowlanders are shouting warnings to their comrades. All their gear is on the machine. They'll be stranded if they lose it.

Suddenly the cable goes slack and you hear a scraping noise from above.

"It's off," you yell. "Cut the cable!"

Piver grabs a pair of cutters from his belt and bears down on the cable. With a *ping* it separates from the drum.

The scraping is getting louder.

"Geebus, I hope it doesn't take us out on its way past," Piver squeaks, nervously.

So do you, but there is nothing you can do about that now.

Whoosh! The machine slides by before you even see it coming.

"Whoa that was close," Piver says.

Piver's teeth sparkle in the dark.

"Well done, miners. I'm proud of you," the officer says. "That's one machine that won't be roaming the Highlands any time soon."

You must admit you're a little proud of yourself too. Sliders will sing songs of this encounter for many years to come. You and Piver have etched a place in slider history, even though you're only miners.

"Okay troops, the sun will be up in less than an hour. Let's get out of here."

"What will happen to the Lowlanders?" you ask.

"We'll send some sliders for them in a day or two. They'll be very happy to surrender after a couple of cold nights on the slopes.

The climb back down is easier. With a series of belays, you and the sliders make your way down to the Pillars. By the time you are standing outside the main portal, the sun is climbing over the ridge.

It's another beautiful day on the Black Slopes.

"Hey," Piver says. "Where do you find a group of Lowlanders when they've lost one of their fancy machines?"

It's a bit early in the morning for jokes, but you're in a good mood. "I don't know. Where?"

"Exactly where you left them!"

Congratulations, you and Piver have saved the day. Later that month you were both awarded the Highland Medal of Bravery and made honorary members of the Slider Corps. The sliders even let you keep your guide sticks.

But have you followed all the possible paths this book has to offer? Have you encountered morph rats? Found the secret of the moon moths?

It's time for you to make another decision. Do you:

Go back to the very beginning of the story and try another path? **P1**

Or

Go to the list of choices and start reading from another part of the story? **P216**

You have decided to stay quiet and let the sliders plan their attack from above

You are hesitant to tell the sliders how to do their job, even though you think that sneaking up from below might be the right thing to do.

The slider officer has gathered his troop together to discuss strategy. You move a little closer so you can hear what they are saying.

"We'll have to wait until morning," the officer says. "Trying to get above the Lowlanders at night would be too dangerous with a couple miners in tow."

You watch the Lowlanders through your scope as you listen in on the sliders' conversation.

"But if we wait till morning, we may never catch them in time," another slider grumps.

You think a moment. "Wait, I have an idea."

"And what might that be?" the officer growls, angry at having his thinking interrupted.

"What if Piver and I climbed up the machine's track to the Lowland camp, while you and your troop go up and around? If you distract the Lowlanders from above, it will give us time to hook a cable onto to their machine and pull them off."

"You think you two can handle that on your own?" the officer asks, a little surprised.

"Climbing the track will be easy. The holes will give us all the hand and footholds we need. The winch we need to pull them off is heavy, but we won't have as far to go as you sliders so we can take a few breaks during the climb."

The officer looks at his team. Many of the sliders are nodding their heads.

"Okay, that's the plan then. You two will have one hour after dewfall to get your equipment in place. When we attack, you'll need to move right away. There is always a chance the Lowlanders will retreat behind their machine. If that happens they will see you for sure."

"Just go easy on them for the first few minutes of your attack. That's all it will take for me to hook a cable on that steaming contraption of theirs," you say. "After that, you can do whatever you like."

Everyone seems happy with the strategy. The Highland sliders adjust their gear and get a few extra anchor bolts out of their packs.

"Good luck," the office says. "Remember, exactly one hour after dewfall."

You wave as the sliders head off. It will be hard climb time for them. Still, that is what they've trained for.

Unlike the sliders who are climbing the long way around, you and Piver waste no time getting ready to take a gentle slide across the valley to the point where you will intersect the track made by the Lowland machine.

The winch is broken down into two parts, with Piver taking the drum of heavy cable while you take the motor and mounting.

The valley is in shadow. Dewfall is less than an hour away

by the time the two of you point your boots slightly downhill and get ready to push off towards the other side of the valley.

"Let's keep as quiet as we can," you say to Piver. "We don't want the Lowlanders to know we're below them.

Piver grins. "Not wrong there. It could get tricky if they start throwing rocks."

With a grim determination, the two of you start your slide. The wind in your face is cooler now that the sun has disappeared behind the ridge. Everywhere you look it is a duller shade of black now that there is no light reflecting off the surface of the slope. Were it not for the flickering lights of the Lowlanders' camp, you would never have known they were there.

You are almost upon the track when you see the series of holes running along the slope. "Here it is," you say to Piver. "Let's get an anchor in and a sling rigged before dewfall. Once it's fully dark, we can start climbing."

You and Piver only get half an hour's rest before the light is gone completely. The night is still, and the only sounds are the odd rattle and voices from the Lowland camp.

"Steady as we go," you say to Piver. "This rock is slipperier than the slime on a morph rat's back."

Standing with your toes jammed into holes, the two of you tighten your packs and rope yourselves together.

"Only one of us moves at a time," you say. "A brief tug on the rope will signal that I'm ready for you to move up."

Piver chuckles nervously, jams his guide stick firmly into a hole and braces himself, ready to hang on should you fall. "Well you'd better get going then," he says.

You sling your stick over your shoulder, stretch forward, and place a fist in each hole. Once your hands are secure you take a few steps. You repeat this process until you're fifteen or so yards further up the slope before jamming your stick in a hole to belay Piver. Giving the cable a light tug, you signal him to climb up to join you. The two of you repeat this procedure until you are only twenty yards at most below the Lowland camp.

"Quiet," you whisper.

Setting up the winch in absolute silence, in the dark, is even trickier than you thought it would be. Luckily there aren't many moving parts, and most of the assembly can be done by feel. Attaching the winch firmly to the slope with expansion bolts is the hardest part. Thankfully the holes in the track save you from having to drill your own. By the time the job is finished, both you and Piver are sweating.

"When the sliders attack, I'm going to drag that cable up the last few yards and shackle it onto their machine as fast as I can," you say.

Piver smiles. "Then I start the winch and drag the morph-heads off," Piver whispers, his teeth gleaming in the dark.

"Exactly," you say. "Just make sure you give me time to get out of the way before you turn it on. Oh and don't forget to cut the cable once they're off. Otherwise it will swing the machine in your direction and..."

"Squish, splat. I get it."

You tap Piver on the arm and throw the cable over your shoulder. "I'm going to get a little closer," you whisper. "The sliders attack should start any moment now."

With your belly close to the ground, you slowly work your way up the track until you are lying only yards away from the platform where the Lowlanders are camped. You are so close to the camp, you can hear the Lowlanders farting around their burners as they eat their beans and mash.

All is black around you until a slice of moon pokes its head above the western ridge of a mountain in the distance. You're please to have a little more light, but hope the diversion the sliders are going to create happens soon, otherwise you might get spotted. When you look down the mountain you can just make out Piver's silhouette against the slope. Moonlight reflects off his teeth, and you wish for once the plucky fellow would stop smiling.

Time moves slowly. Your heart pounds. Thump thump — thump thump — thump thump.

When you hear a yell from above, you are relieved. Within a few moments the entire hillside is alive. Moon shadows stretch across the mountain as the Lowlanders respond to the Highland attack.

You stand in a half crouch and move up the track. Before you know it you are on flattish ground and reaching to steady yourself against the rear of the machine. You need to move forward so you can attach the cable at the front where the winch will have a chance of pulling the machine's sprocket wheel out of its holes and send it tumbling down the mountainside.

The Lowland voices seem further away. The sliders must be drawing them up the slope, as they pretend to retreat.

You work your way forward, feeling for protrusions to grip on to as you go. Then you see a bracket sticking out of the side of the machine near its front left corner. It is a perfect place to attach the cable.

The shackle only takes a moment to attach. Once done, you clip on to the cable and start back down towards Piver, sliding fast. The sound of fighting above is getting closer. The Highlanders must be on the charge again.

You know that if your plan doesn't work, the sliders will fight to the death to defeat this machine.

"Winch!" you yell out to Piver. "Quickly!"

You hear the familiar whine of the motor as it takes up the slack in the cable. The winch strains at its mountings. There is a torturous scrape of metal on stone from above as the machine's front end is dragged around side-on to the slope.

Then the cable goes slack.

"It's off." you say to Piver. "Quick, cut the cable."

Piver grabs a pair of cutters from his belt and bears down on the cable. With a *ping* it separates from the drum.

The scraping and clanking is getting closer.

"I hope it doesn't take us out on its way past," Piver squeaks.

So do you, but there is nothing you can do about that now.

Whoosh! A dark shadow skids by within feet of where you and Piver are standing.

"Geebus! That was close," Piver says.

The fighting rages on for another ten minutes or so, but without their machine the Lowlanders are no match for the Highland Slider Corps. A couple of times you hear someone yell as they plummet down the slope past you in the darkness. You can't tell if they are Highlanders or Lowlanders. Regardless, mothers will weep and families will grieve.

Suddenly, it's like someone's turned off a switch and everything goes silent.

"I wonder who won?" Piver says.

It doesn't take long for you to find out.

"Hey, you miners still alive down there?" a familiar voice calls out.

"Yes." Piver replies.

The two of you climb up the path to the small plateau where the sliders have the Lowlanders sitting in a group with their hands tied together. This is the first time you've seen Lowlanders up close. They look remarkably like members of your own family.

"Well done, you two," the officer says. "As soon as their machine was off, they gave up reasonably easily."

"So what now?" you ask.

"We'll wait until morning and then take them down to the Pillars. They'll get to go home again once their relatives have paid the ransom."

You're pleased that the Lowlanders won't be locked up forever. They don't look much older than you.

"Oh and by the way," the officer says to you and Piver. "I'm going to recommend that you and funny boy here are made honorary sliders."

"Geebus!" Piver says. "Real sliders?"

"Yes," the officer says, "real Highland sliders. Assuming you don't trip and go to the bottom on the way home that is."

For once, your grin is as wide as Piver's. Your family will be so pleased. Now you can follow your dream to be a miner, while being a slider too.

Congratulation, you have finished this part of the story. But have you tried all the different paths? Have you found the moon moth's secret chamber and fought the morph rats? Have you explored the old mine shaft and discovered the reservoir? It is time for you to make another decision. Do you:

Go back to the very beginning of the story and try another path? **P1**

Or

Go to the list of choices and start reading from another part of the story? **P216**

You have decided to carry on to the Pillars of Haramon with the Lowlanders' message.

You are pleased the sliders have left the decision up to you and are ready to continue on to the Pillars of Haramon with the Lowlanders' message. To start a war without the Highland Council discussing the matter would be irresponsible and put many lives at risk.

What if the Lowlanders really do have some new technology that would make fighting them pointless? Maybe joining their federation would bring benefits to your community. Whichever the case, the Highland Council will have to decide which course of action to take.

"Well if we're not fighting, we'd better get sliding," the head slider says. "We've still got a lot of rock to cover if we're going to get to the Pillars before dewfall."

You tell the miners to check their loads and climb aboard their sledges.

"Any objection if we take the fast route to the Pillars?" the slider officer asks. "I'm assuming this message is urgent."

"Do what you need to, as long as we get there in one piece," you say.

The officer reorganizes his troop for fast travel, one slider steering and two braking on each sledge.

You cinch your waist strap tight and get ready for a speedy ride.

"This should be fun," Piver yells over to you. "I've always

wanted to be on a sledge with a bunch of crazy sliders going at top speed down the mountainside. NOT!"

You know how he feels, but you also know that the council will need time to discuss the Lowlanders' offer. The more time they have, the better decision they are likely to make.

"On my mark!" the officer yells.

And with a jerk of the sledge you're off.

The fast route zigzags down a steep face then cuts across a ridge into Long Gully. Further down Long Gully are the Pillars of Haramon, one of the Highland's most secure outposts.

As your slider escorts guide you down the mountain track, you look around at the scenery. Far below is a wonderful mosaic of color. To the west, dark brooding mountains march off into the haze.

"Here comes the tricky part," Shoola calls as your sledge screeches around a hairpin bend.

You look off to the side of your sledge and see only air.

"Geebus that's steep!" you hear Piver shout from the sledge behind you.

He's not wrong. You swallow hard and hold on a little tighter. Looking down makes you feel a little queasy. You look out over the ranges and pretend you're on a simulator. Only unlike the simulators at mining school, this one has a stiff breeze blowing in your face and the screech of sliders straining on their hooks to slow the sledge down for the corners.

When your group finally gets to the bottom, you breathe a sigh of relief. Once they've skirted a small crevasse field, the sliders turn the sledges onto a small plateau and stop.

"You have ten minutes," the leader says.

While most of the sliders sit to rest their legs, the miners are off their sledges a quickly as possible to attach tethers and then stretch. Hydro bars are unwrapped as some have a quick snack.

The bone rattling ride down the mountain has made you need to pee, so you move away from the group and duck behind a small rocky outcrop about twenty yards from the main group.

Just as you start to loosen your uniform, you hear the slurping feet and gnashing teeth of morph rats. Apart from an unexpected cloud burst, this is the most dreaded sound in all the Highlands.

"Morph rats!" you yell, forgetting all about your need to pee.

You look up the slope and can't believe you eyes. There must be a thousand of the horrible creatures, and they are heading in your direction. Their slimy bodies are a light green and the suckers on their feet slurp with every step they take on the slippery black rock.

As they get closer, the clattering of their teeth gets louder. These teeth can strip a full-grown pango to nothing but bone in less than a minute.

Feral packs eat anything in their path. Thankfully, their sense of smell and eyesight are really bad. You can fight them or hide from them.

You need to make a decision quickly. Do you:

Climb up on top of the rocky outcrop and hope the morph rats go around you? **P202**

Or

Run back over to the others and fight the morph rats as a group? **P205**

You have decided to climb on top of the rocky outcrop.

You're not sure that you have time to get to the others before the morph rats are upon you, so you start climbing up the rock. With a bit of luck, the pack of morph rats will stream around you and continue blindly on down the slope.

Their slurping footsteps are getting closer, their teeth chattering like pebbles tumbling down the mountainside.

"Sliders! Uphill V formation now! Miners, get in behind!" you hear a slider yell.

From your vantage point on the rock, you see the sliders bunch together, each has turned their pack around to the front to protect their chest. Their guide sticks, with diamond hooks to the front, are tucked firmly under their armpits, while both hands hold firmly onto the shaft.

The miners are behind the sliders' formation, hand picks up and at the ready.

The pack of morph rats move like a writhing wave of teeth and slime down the hillside.

When the wave hits, those at the point of the V-formation will sweep the rats to the side using their sticks.

"Try to flip the rats onto their backs so they lose their grip on the slope," the head slider says. "That way, by the time they regain their feet they'll be too far down the mountain to be of any danger."

The clicking and slurping sends a chill down your spine. One slip and everyone is rat food.

You don't have your pick with you. You left it leaning

against your sledge when you headed for the rock. That was a big mistake.

Without your pick, all you can do is hope the rats go around the rock rather than over it. If any rats do decide to climb towards your position you just hope you'll be able to kick them away.

You watch with a morbid fascination as the wave of slimy flesh and pointed teeth surges towards your rock. Anyone that ends up in this seething mass of animals won't last long.

The sliders stand with sticks at the ready.

All you can do is watch and wait.

When the mass of rat flesh reaches your position, the sheer weight of rats behind the front of the wave, pushes rats up the rock you are standing on. The first few you manage to kick off, but before long your boots are covered in slime and standing on the rock is becoming more difficult.

You chance a quick glance at the others and see that the sliders' technique is working. The wave of rats is parting around the sliders and miners on the slope.

You feel teeth dig into your shin and try to kick the rats at your feet away, but slime is all over your rock now. You try another kick, but lose your balance. You are falling into the swarm.

Unfortunately this part of your adventure is over. You made the mistake of thinking you could escape the morph rats by climbing the rock. You should have gone back and joined forces with the others. There is always safety in numbers when it comes to fighting off an enemy.

It is now time for you to make another decision. Do you:

Go back to the very beginning of the story and try another path? **P1**

Or

Go back to your last choice and choose differently? **P205**

You have decided to run back over to the others and fight the morph rats off as a group.

"Sliders, uphill-V-formation, quickly! You miners tuck in behind," the head slider yells.

You move as fast as you can to where the sliders are forming into a defensive position to take on the advancing wave of morph rats.

The rat's slurping footsteps are getting closer. Their teeth clatter and click as they move.

The sliders bunch together. Each has turned their pack around to protect their chest from the rat's razor-sharp teeth, should one of them break through. Their guide sticks, with diamond hooks pointing to the front, are tucked under their armpits. They clutch the shaft firmly in both hands. Grim determination is set in their eyes.

You and the other miners squeeze in behind the sliders' formation, hand picks at the ready.

The pack of morph rats moves like a writhing wave of teeth and slime down the hillside towards you. It isn't a pretty sight, and smells even worse.

When the wave of rats reaches the V-formation, the sliders at the front furiously sweep the rats to each side using their sticks like brooms. The sliders near the rear of the group then try to flip the rats onto their backs so they lose their grip on the slope and slide too far down the mountain to be of any danger.

"Geebus, look at them!" Piver shivers in disgust, his pick

at the ready. "They have got to be the ugliest creatures alive."

Snap, click, snap go thousands of teeth.

"Ugh, I can smell their breath from here," Piver says. "It's like rotten eggs."

The sliders are struggling to sweep aside the writhing mass as it slurps past.

"Yeow!" a miner yelps as a morph rat chomps onto his leg. He swings his pick knocking the rat out and then kicks the hideous creature down the slope. "That hurt!"

And then, as suddenly as they came, the rats have passed, slithering further down the slope in search of plump pangos.

"Well done sliders," the officer says. "Never get isolated by morph rats, if you do, you're better off free sliding. Being swarmed by morph rats is not the way you want to go, believe me."

You see Piver close his eyes and shudder. Sometimes his overactive imagination leads to funny situations, at other times it can be a curse.

"You okay Piver?" you ask. He looks a little pale.

"Yeah, it's just that…" He shakes his head. "Never mind, I don't want to think about it."

"Right, load up," the head slider says. "We've got to get to the Pillars before dewfall."

Remembering you needed to pee, you rush back over behind the rock and relieve yourself. The rock is covered in rat slime. If you'd stayed there you wouldn't have survived.

After everyone is ready your little caravan sets off again,

moving at top speed towards the Pillars of Haramon.

"Cute little critters those rats, eh?" Shoola says as she slides down the mountain behind you.

"Yeah right," you say. "Ever eaten one?"

"Just once. My troop was trapped high up the mountain in a storm. All we could do for six days was anchor ourselves on the mountain and hang on. By the time it was safe to move around, we hadn't eaten in three days."

"Three days?"

"We were just about to slide off, when a small pack of rats came by. Let's just say it was messy. By the time we'd skinned a couple, there was slime everywhere. I can still smell it in my uniform some days."

You can't imagine not eating for three days. But even then, you don't know if you'd ever get hungry enough to eat a morph rat. "Yuck. Sounds horrible."

Shoola smiles. "Let's just say I've taken dumps that smelled better and leave it at that."

You laugh and look out over the valley. The sun is getting low in the sky. Soon it will disappear behind the ridge and the temperature will drop six or seven degrees. An hour after that, dewfall will start. You just hope you've arrived at the Pillars by then.

About forty minutes later, you see two towering monoliths rising high above the valley floor in the distance. The black stone pillars are the most beautiful sight you have ever seen. Smooth and shining, they dwarf everything around them. Sunshine still illuminates their tops.

You want to make some comment to Shoola about how amazing they look, but your mouth is hanging open in awe and any words you come up with seem inadequate.

"Not far now," she says.

Within ten minutes your caravan is outside one of the Pillar's main portals. A door slides open at its base and the sliders maneuver the sledges inside a cavern hollowed out of the solid rock.

With a hiss of air, the massive doors close again and you unbuckle your straps.

"Welcome to the Pillars of Haramon," a crew member says. "Cutting it a bit fine for dewfall weren't you?"

The head slider steps forward. "Considering we ran into Lowlanders and a huge swarm of morph rats, I think we've done well just to make it here in one piece."

You and the other miners mumble your agreement.

"I need to get a message to the Highland Council," you say. "The Lowlanders have given us an ultimatum."

"You'd better go up to the command pod and tell the officer in charge. Ultimatums are above my pay grade."

The crew member points you towards a spiral staircase cut into the rock. "They're on the top floor."

"You mean I've got to climb a thousand feet to the top of the Pillars?" This is not what you had in mind.

"No, silly. There's a cable-lift two flights up."

You breathe a sigh of relief and start up the first flight. You wonder how big each flight is and start counting. The first flight is 39 steps. By the time you reach the landing you are sweating. "I must do more exercise," you tell yourself.

At the top of the second flight, you come to a place where a vertical shaft has been bored into the rock. A motorized cable runs up the tunnel. Every five seconds or so, a sturdy platform appears. You watch as a slider steps onto a platform and is whisked up the tunnel. Now it's just a matter of timing your step. After counting and watching for a minute, you feel you've got it worked out and prepare to step aboard.

"Five, four, three, two, one, step," you count.

For a split second you think you've made a mistake, but then you feel something solid beneath your feet. Your knees bend slightly and you are plunged into darkness as you rise up the shaft.

"But how do I get off?" you mumble to yourself. "I should have asked someone."

Your hand tightens around the cable. You can feel it vibrating as you climb. Every fifty feet or so, you move past an opening and can see out of the shaft into what must have been mine workings many years ago. Now they are just empty chambers, with ventilation holes overlooking the valley below.

You hear voices from above. The top can't be far away. Light is starting to penetrate down the shaft from above and the sound of a drum whirling the cable back down is getting louder.

An opening appears. You jump.

Your landing in the command pod isn't graceful, but at

least you've made it. You hear chuckling and see three slider officers looking at you.

"Welcome miner," one of the men says. "You have a message for us I believe."

"Yes, for the Highland Council."

"Well spit it out."

You look at the slider officer. "Are you on the council?"

The officer looks down at the three cut diamonds pinned to his chest. "See those stars?"

You nod.

"Know what they mean?"

You shake your head.

"It means I'm chief of the Highland Council. Don't they teach that at mining school these days?"

"Sorry, no," you say, a little embarrassed.

"Well come on. What's the message?"

You give him the message about joining the Lowland Federation. You tell him about the offer of education and healthcare … and the tax. You also tell him about the Lowlanders' threat, and how the one you spoke to seemed extremely confident in their new technology.

The council chief's face takes on a stony appearance as he considers what you've said. "Our spies have seen these machines. But I can't imagine the members of the council agreeing to the Lowlanders' terms. Highlanders have been fiercely independent for generations and we don't take kindly to threats."

"But what about the healthcare, education and other

benefits they offer?" you ask. "Aren't they worth considering?"

"We have education."

"Not a very good education it seems."

The chief scowls at you. "I'm not sure I like your tone."

"Why can't we talk peace?" you say. "Do we have to keep this hatred going just out of pride?" You look up into the chief's brooding face. "How many will die in this war? All of us?"

The chief isn't used to people standing up to him. He stomps his foot and snarls like he's about to bite his tongue off and spit it at you. "How dare you!"

You take a step back as spittle flies in your direction. The man is grinding his teeth and growling like a wild animal. "Sliders never surrender!"

"And in my family we never enter a fight unless we know we can win!"

This makes the chief pause. He harrumphs and walks to the far side of the pod and looks out the window at the shadowed slopes below. It seems an age before he turns around and faces you.

"Do you really think we could lose everything?"

"I don't know," you say. "But even if there is the slightest chance of that happening, is it worth the risk? And if by some stroke of luck we do come out on top, how many of your friends will die in the process?"

Once again the chief's face turns to stone. You can almost see him thinking. "You're pretty plucky for a miner," he says a minute or so later.

"I come from generations of sliders, remember."

Finally you get a little smile from the chief. "Okay, get back to your pod. I'll speak to the council and see what they say."

When you arrive back at the accommodation pod, the others are eating. You grab some broth and take it over to sit with Piver and Shoola.

"So what's up?" Piver asks.

You fill them in on your meeting with the council chief.

"You think they'll talk peace?" Piver asks. "It would be the first time in three generations."

"I don't know. I just hope that the council can see the bigger picture. Life is tough enough on the slopes without having to fight all the time."

"I have a cousin who is a Lowlander," Shoola says.

"Really?" Piver asks. "How did that happen?"

"He just slid off one day and disappeared. Seems he'd met a girl from one of the border tribes during a trade meeting and fell in love."

Piver's eyes grew wide. "And he never came back?"

"He did some years later. Tried to tell everyone that the Lowlanders were just like us, but the people in the communities wouldn't listen."

"So what happened?" you ask.

"He had no choice but to go back down the mountain. It broke his family's heart."

The three of you sit in silence for a while, sipping your

broth, lost in your own thoughts.

"Just like us?" Piver finally said.

Shoola nodded.

Piver looked confused. "Then why are we fighting them?"

Shoola shrugged her shoulders. "I think it's been so long, everyone has forgotten why we started."

Later, you think about what Shoola has said as you fall asleep on your bunk.

The next morning you are awoken by someone shaking your shoulder.

"What?"

"Come with me," a slider says. "Chief wants a word."

You get up and dress quickly. The slider leads you towards the cable-lift.

When the two of you reach the command pod there are twelve people sitting around a large table.

The chief waves you to a seat near one end. "Please sit."

You wonder what is going on. Everyone is looking at you.

The chief clears his throat. "This is the young miner I told you about."

Eleven faces swivel towards you.

The chief looks in your direction. "We've sent a delegation to talk peace with the Lowlanders. They left at first light this morning."

You can't help but think they've done the right thing.

An older woman stands up and walks towards your seat. She places her withered hands on your shoulders. "I am an old woman, but I know a clever mind and a good heart when I see one."

You look up into her clear green eyes.

"I want you to take my seat on the council young miner. We need new blood. Blood untarnished by years of conflict."

Is she talking about you joining the council? Surely not. What experience do you have?

"But…"

"Quiet," the old woman says. "It's time the council heard the truth. And you, young as you are, are the first person to give it to them."

"If the Highlands are to prosper, we need to stop putting so many of our resources into fighting the Lowlanders. Joining The Federation of Lowland States might be just the opportunity we are looking for."

Heads around the table are nodding in agreement.

"So do you accept the appointment?" the chief says to you.

"I … I'm a bit…"

"Surprised?" the chief says

"Geebus!" you say, using Piver's favorite exclamation. "Now there's the understatement of the century."

A light chuckle runs around the table.

"So what do you say?" the old woman asks. "Will you help us steer the Highlands towards peace?"

You think for a moment and search the faces before you.

"Well ?" the chief says. "Are you up to the job?"

You think about your family and how proud they would

be if you were to become a member of the council. How their disappointment at you deciding to become a miner rather than a slider would wash away like pango droppings in a heavy rain.

"Of course I'm up for it. I come from good slider stock remember?"

Congratulations, this part of your story is over. You successfully helped start the peace process on your planet and became a member of the Highland Council, a great honor to you and your family. Well done! But have you followed all the possible paths yet? Have you gone to slider school? Gone down into a scary cave? Been caught in a storm?

It is now time to make another decision. Do you:

Go back to the very beginning of the story and try a different path? **P1**

Or

Go to the list of choices and start reading from another part of the story? **P216**

List of Choices

Yell out for the slider not to attack. 150

Tell the officer he should talk peace with Lowlanders. 154

Volunteer to help attack the Lowland machine. 157

Leave the Pillars and strike out for home. 169

Suggest an attack from below. 183

Stay quiet. Let the sliders plan their attack from above 190

Carry on to the Pillars with the Lowlanders' message. 198

Climb on top of the rocky outcrop. 202

Fight the morph rats as a group. 205

More You Say Which Way Adventures

Pirate Island

Volcano of Fire

Between the Stars

Once Upon an Island

In the Magician's House

Secrets of Glass Mountain

Danger on Dolphin Island

The Sorcerer's Maze - Jungle Trek

The Sorcerer's Maze - Adventure Quiz

YouSayWhichWay.com

Printed in Great Britain
by Amazon